The Consequent

Stephanie Layton

Published by Haunted Mauve LLC, 2025.

Author's Note

This novel is a compilation of ghost stories by someone who has a few real ones and knows there are many others who have experiences of their own. It is for those others that this story was put together, that while this work is fiction, it may provide comfort and conviction of the truths we carry.

Like any ghostly or paranormal story, there isn't a full explanation for all the bumps in the night. Brace yourself for that now. How could there ever be a full explanation this side of the veil?

Tread softly. Pray heartily. Carry yourself well. Be encouraged in faith. You are not alone.

—to Christ be the glory in all things—

For now we see in a mirror dimly, but then face to face, now I know in part, but then I will know fully, just as I also have been fully known. 1 Corinthians 13:12

Prologue

November 30, 2022

Hamish felt backlit and unseen. The softly papered, champagne-tinted walls were muffed by gold lit candelabras. They lined the crowded lobby beneath small chandeliers, which hung in a glowing canopy of hushed light. He had been waiting at the check-in for several minutes within the hustle and bustle of patrons and clerks and had yet to be acknowledged. His black, formal attire complete with a cream rose boutonniere did not help him to stand out among the rush of guests in similar clothing. There were a few patrons wearing jeans, clearly not in town for the same event. When formal events are your business, you tend to dress the part.

Hamish shifted his weight. He'd been leaning heavy on his left foot for too long. Three hours in the car had him wanting to alleviate the right one. He had arrived dressed for the social welcome event and celebratory speech that was to take place that evening and had been relieved to receive a text about an hour before arrival with the cancellation of the speaker. Social hour was still on, but he did not plan to attend.

Having rung the golden bell on the counter twice, several minutes apart, with no one having come to his aide, he did not really want to ring it again. It felt futile. Instead, Hamish decided to wait a few more minutes and then perhaps walk behind the counter and stop a passing clerk in their tracks. He hypothesized standing before them and refusing to move.

It was all so unusual. He had stayed at many hotels and many less *nice* than this one but never encountered anything like the way this bustling place was drowning him out. Patrons on either side of him had been checked in and given room keys. They had been given instructions on check-out, advice on local restaurants, and maps of the town that quite frankly seemed too small to need a map. He wiggled his toes, the still slightly numb ones of the left foot, and watched a bellman collect the luggage and parcels from a family that had just arrived.

At last a young woman in a clerk's vest and high button shirt came and stood before him, making eye contact. "Have you been helped sir?" she asked from across the check-in desk.

"No," he replied. "Checking in though, Hamish Blackwood."

She apologized for the wait and pulled his name up in the system. She mumbled something he couldn't quite catch and thanked him for his patience. Then she took off down the length of the long check-in desk and disappeared into a door at the end of the long wall behind it. At this juncture, he put his elbows down on the slightly raised portion of the desk in front of him and rested his head on his hands. The room went strangely quiet as he did so. He was still aware of the crowds around him, of their movement, and of the fact that they were making noise, yet unable to exactly hear them. He heard instead a blustery tune that he presumed was coming from the lobby speakers. Figuring that he hadn't been aware of it over all the noise, he didn't take it to be something new. A little like a muted bugle in a thunderstorm, oddly serene and swelling with divots, little pools of piano, it played thoroughly loud enough that he wasn't sure how he had missed it even with the din of the lobby.

It gave him a strange sensation.

The clerk returned as quickly as she had gone, with a taller, male counterpart. He nodded and smiled at Hamish, leaned over the computer screen, and sighed, "Ah, well. We are full."

"I booked a room months ago, back in May," Hamish protested, lifting himself up off his elbows.

The man nodded. "Yes, sir. You have a room."

They stared at each other a moment. He looking rather resigned and Hamish looking rather unsure at what the man was saying.

"Have a good stay sir. Clara will finish checking you in." And he was off. Clara and Hamish watched him walk to the end of the desk and enter the door she had procured him from.

"What was that about?" he asked as they turned to face each other.

"Oh, just a busy night, sir. You know. The convention and all," she replied, darting her eyes down to the screen and typing away. She said nothing else until she handed him his room key. She looked at it and looked at him. He looked at it and looked at her.

"Room 400," she said. "It's a corner unit."

Having had a long day of work prior to his long drive, he was thankful enough to have a key to a room and thankful to be able to escape the bustle of the lobby. He nodded goodbye without giving any further inquiry and headed toward the elevators which he had seen off to the side on his way in. He figured he'd go to the room and look it over before bringing in his suitcase. He had just one piece of luggage as he wasn't staying more than two nights but thought he had better be sure about wanting to bring it in at all, even though he was eager to get settled.

The elevator doors glinted with the same gold opulence of the lobby lights, fixtures, and wallpaper. They were framed in the wall with scrolled trim, also gold or something plated with gold that bent around the doorframe. It was sculpted as a swooping ribbon held at the top by doves that could easily have been mistaken for boars with tusks stretching too far outside their heads. The call button was already lit to the right of a slightly hunched woman in a woven floral overcoat with sparse, but curly hair. Hamish waited behind her. She glanced at him, smiled faintly, and turned back to the doors when he returned her smile with his.

A moment later the doors opened, revealing red, carpeted walls within and immediately he became aware of the music. It was the same he had heard while waiting for Clara to return. It hovered blithely and hoarded the air around his ears, each swell pocked with a divot. It rolled. He felt faintly nauseas. The woman in the floral overcoat stepped aside as a group of three exited the elevator. She glanced at Hamish again, who took a slight bow and motioned for her to go first. She entered and pushed the button for the fifth floor. He pushed the one for the fourth. The doors shut and the music played on. About the time they started to sweep past floor two, the music altered in texture, becoming tangibly gritty.

"Strange music, isn't it?" he said, looking over at the woman.

She gave him a startled and weary glance. Grimacing a little, she said, "It's just the Bee Gees," then shrugged her hunched shoulders and let out a sigh.

Taken aback, but also amused by her reply, he stifled a laugh. Hamish had four Bee Gees albums at home. This was not the Bee Gees.

"You don't hear a weird trumpety, organ type song— like, I don't know, maybe the instruments have sand in their teeth?" he asked.

She shook her head and drew her coat tighter around her shoulders. The elevator doors opened, and he stepped out without looking back.

The fourth-floor hall was silent. For that, he was thankful. He looked for a placard telling him which way to go, but there were none to be seen. A room door in front of him, slightly to the left read 411 in brass numerals and to the right was a small enclave with benches and what appeared to be a little snack station with a pastry basket, as well as a basket for fruit, which at the moment held a single apple. The hall stretched past the enclave and ended a significant way down with the option to turn left or right. The first room door in that direction read 420. Not really thinking much about what happened to rooms 412-419, he took a left and headed away from the enclave towards where he hoped room 400 would be. The hall in this direction also turned optionally to the left or right. Just before the left turn he found his corner unit, the room on the inner edge.

Compared to the lobby and even to the elevator, the décor in the hall had not been much to consider. It was relatively plain and neutral. The oak, tiger striped wood grain doors to the rooms were stained a rich brown with brass room numbers, room 400 being the exception. The door of 400 was oak, tiger striped wood grain. It was stained a rich brown. The room numbers, however, were not brass. They were frosted and quartz-like. Touching their cool surface, trying to decide what they were made of Hamish just about hurled an expletive when a woman with softly blonde hair and a light silvery blouse rounded the corner and nearly knocked him down. Instead he jumped forward and banged into the door.

The woman apologized profusely, for which there wasn't really a need, Hamish told her. He was fine. They had a laugh and then the woman went down to the enclave and Hamish went back to staring at the frosted numerals on his door until out of the corner of his eye, he saw the woman reemerge with the apple. They exchanged a friendly nod. The woman raised the apple in a toast and headed off in the other direction.

Not having decided on the material of the numbers, Hamish held the room key up to the scanner on the door. It was one of those plastic things the size of a credit card, with the hotel's name and logo printed across one side. In this case it was a purple plume with *Inventes* spelled out in a blue, ribbon like font. The scanner lit green, and the door slid smoothly open with a turn of the handle. He looked back down the hall to see if he could still see the woman with the softly blonde hair and silvery blouse, but she had gone.

There was darkness. Pushing the door fully open, allowing enough light from the hall to show him the switch to his right, he gave it a flip. The bulb stuttered a little before settling in a soft yellow above the entryway. The entryway was just a tiny hall with a coat rack on the left just before the bathroom door, a mirror to the right next to the light switch, then a couple feet till it opened up into the rest of the room. The center of the room featured a thistle and plum hued rug, with what appeared to be a full-size bed on top of it with an oak headboard against the left wall. A nightstand and a floor lamp tethered each side. Across from the bed was a small dresser with a small television. On top of the television was a digital clock the size of a toddler's shoe and the remote.

Everything in the room seemed too small for the space. The shade on a tall window at the back of the room was pulled down to the frame, but the set of lace eyelet curtains were too short to reach the frame and ended awkwardly about a foot above it. He had never recalled thinking such a thing about curtains before, that they could be awkward, but these were. The whole room was.

However, it seemed clean. A quick inspection of the bathroom found it to be in working order with a lingering scent of bleach. There was no overhead light in the main area, but the floor lamps worked with a subdued quality. The shade for the window opened easily, revealing an atrium courtyard that allowed for a smidge more light. The bed looked comfortable and appeared to be free of bedbugs, which he always checked for no matter where he stayed. Honestly, he couldn't see what the strangeness at the desk had been about, unless it was simply that the room itself was strange. Beyond the furniture being small for the space there was a something or other about it that just felt wrong.

Perhaps because the lighting was lacking, or maybe because it had been a long day and he was really very tired, whatever the reason, the wrongness of the room felt as if maybe it was coming in slant ways, off kilter, off balance from just out of his periphery.

Hamish walked back to the window and looked out into the courtyard. The atrium below was filled with trees, ferns with large fronds, and orchids in an array of purples and pinks. There were even a couple of streetlamps and benches. Across the way was an identical looking brick section of the hotel with windows to other rooms overlooking the atrium. These two identical sides were attached by frosted glass walls to the left and to the right. The color of the glass reminded Hamish of a thistle he had once found encased in ice. Within these wave-riddled glass walls, set in iron framework along the edges, at the height of the fourth floor, were singular, horizontal brick stripes. He reckoned the stripes were the fourth-floor halls connecting the two brick sides of the hotel together. These brick sections were tall enough and long enough to be the exterior of the hallway walls. The dark sky was visible through a rounded glass roof that arched above, uniting all the sides.

Making up his mind that he would go and get his luggage before the night progressed any further, he turned away from the window when his legs completely buckled and tumbling forward, he attempted to catch himself on the edge of the bed. There was too much space between the bed and the window, however, and he caught just the quilt, and half pulled it into the floor where he landed.

This was new. He had never had his legs collapse out from under him before. Kneeling on the floor with the quilt in his fist, he did not move for several moments. He listened to his pulse. He listened for the strange music. Ultimately, he decided that he was just more tired than he realized and perhaps had a circulation issue considering how numb his foot had been and gave himself another moment before attempting to get up.

When he did rise, his legs were not in any sort of pain. He felt fine, caught off guard, but fine. There was no further trouble in exiting the room. He checked to make sure he had his key and went to retrieve his luggage. The music had vanished from the elevator and if it were playing in the lobby, he couldn't hear it over the continuing bustle of the patrons and employees. He saw a few recognizable faces when making his way back through the lobby—waved—nodded—and kept enough distance so as not to have to fully interact. That would wait until tomorrow. There was no room in his brain at the moment for social etiquette and polite conversations. Throughout this whole venture out and back, he kept testing his knees and legs, with extra bending and stretching of stride. They didn't give any sort of suggestion of a problem. His heartbeat felt steady and his head clear with the exception of being tired.

When he returned and exited the elevator back on the fourth floor, he saw an attendant leaving the enclave with a cart, and caught sight of the baskets, which were now filled. Finding it very appealing that the pastries and fruit would be replenished in the evening and weren't just for breakfast, he decided to pick up something to take back with him having completely forgotten about dinner and having no intention of going back out. Next to the baskets were clear plastic carry-out containers, paper plates, napkins, and paper cups for the coffee and tea stations that he had not been able to see from the hall. He picked out a banana, two blueberry muffins, and a packet of chamomile tea. He filled up a cup with hot water for the tea and went back to the room. At the door, he again found himself staring at the frosted numerals, as he juggled the make-do dinner with his one suitcase in an attempt to get his key out of his pocket. Before he could procure the key, just as he felt the plastic of it on the tips of his fingers, the card sensor clicked, flashed green, and the door handle bent, opening the door just slightly enough for him to see that he had left the entry way light on.

Pushing it the rest of the way open, he glanced around half expecting to see someone else in the room— perhaps by mistake, perhaps for nefarious reasons. He imagined throwing his hot water in their face, should they try anything stupid. There was no one. He checked the shower and under the bed, once he had put down everything except the hot water, which he held at the ready. Once those tedious and suspicious spaces were cleared, Hamish locked the door with the deadbolt and chain. He pulled the window shade down, put his tea into the hot water, relinquished it to a nightstand, lay the rose from his jacket beside it, and took a quick, though slightly paranoid shower.

It was a relief to finally crawl into the bed. With the quilt folded down to the foot, he pulled the other blankets up close and opened the plastic carry out box that he had set down next to himself. Regretting not grabbing the television remote from where it sat on top of the small tv, he resigned himself to watching the digital clock, peeling back the wrapper from one of the blueberry muffins as the clock flashed from 8:00 to 8:01.

It was extremely tasty for a hotel grab and go muffin, being light and airy. The blueberries were fresh too. They didn't seem at all like the sort of preserved, flavorless things that often pervade bulk distributed muffins. These muffins were probably made this evening, and this one was quickly making him forget about the whole awkwardness of the hotel experience thus far.

He finished the first one and the second, and about half the tea, then decided he would save the banana for tomorrow. It was early by his usual evening routine, however, tonight it was sufficiently late enough to sign off on the right to pass into sleep.

He turned off the floor lamps, which could not be reached from the bed, much to his lazied dismay. The room was sufficiently dark and quiet with a soft glow coming in through the sides of the curtained shade from the courtyard streetlamps. The only other light came from the red dot of a bulb on a smoke detector, near the door. Once he lay down, he couldn't even see that.

The sleep he had been anticipating with a great welcome, did not come. No sooner had he started to drift into that space between dreaming and awake when a blaze of blue vibrance filled the space behind his lids. Opening his eyes, now fully alert, he found the room blackened and like it had been when he lay down. He closed his eyes again and once again a blue vibrance broke across his sense of sight, as if someone were setting off flash bombs at the side of the bed. Again, he opened his eyes and found the room dark. This time though, the room had lost its quiet. The same organish, piano pocked song from the lobby and the elevator, returned to him and moved about the bed in swirls of audible motion. It swooped and danced until it lay hovering near the window.

The strangest part of all was that he was sure he was only hearing it in his head, even though he knew he was not producing it from within himself. It was intrusively in his brain space and yet it was from without that psychological firing range from which it swung and moved.

He lay motionless for moments peering into the dark and saw nothing but the shape of the nightstand and its surface contents. Listening, he thought he knew it was near the window, though he did not want to look over. He could not have said exactly how long he lay there, just that it kept playing and he kept listening and trying to discern the true source. At last, he sat up. The music did not stop. It did not soften. He began to wonder if perhaps he had a brain tumor. Perhaps he was ill. He'd had an egg salad sandwich from a gas station for lunch. Maybe the sandwich was bad. His stomach felt fine. It had felt fine all day. He did not even feel tired anymore, just perplexed, but not in any sort of pain. Even his foot was less numb. Oddly, now that he had sat up, he didn't even feel afraid.

The gritty, tighter portion of the song began. At this juncture, he climbed out of bed and put his ear to the wall in case it was coming from the neighboring room, though he knew it was not. Sighing deeply and feeling as though he had no choice, he went to the window, peeked around the side of the shade, and looked out into the courtyard, though he knew before he looked, the source would not be found there either.

Turning back from the window, he was met with the cream rose. It hung in the air before him at eye level. It bowed toward him, gave a spin matching the melody, and fell onto the floor at his feet.

The music ceased. Immediately. Mid-note. Hamish stood in the silence, in the dark, and stared down at the rose. He began to be slightly afraid. He'd had experiences as a child, far worse than this. Those were a long time ago. In comparison, he supposed, this spinning rose, and phantom song should be things he could deal with, even if he did not know how to process them.

Processing was always the hardest part. In moments like these, when it seemed fear should reign, his brain would try so desperately to grasp hold of logic, that fear would falter away in the presence of defiance and shift to wonderment. Defying logic, however, could only distract for so long. Eventually the other half of his brain would kick in—the half that says not to talk to strangers, the half that says to fight or flee—and then all the nerve endings in his body would begin to agree with that instinctive half of his brain. This was when he became afraid, when the wonderment was gone.

He bent down and picked up the rose, running his thumb over the petals as soft as their color. Then he tentatively put it back on the nightstand and hastily placed himself back under the covers. Like a child, he sat there in the dark, wanting someone to come to his aid, to tell him that it was all fine, just his imagination, but he knew it wasn't his imagination. It never had been.

ACT I

Chapter 1

Imagine Shadows Magazine
July 14, 2015
The Consequent
by Morely B.

I no longer find comfort in writing. The more I want to say, the less it wants to be said. Some stories don't like being told and this is one of them. A mentor once told me that my greatest asset was my stubborn nature. Perhaps it is my biggest flaw as I am telling the story whether it wishes to be told, or not. You may refer to me as Morely. I was a community actor at The Consequent, a small theater in the south. The Consequent, of course, is a pseudonym. It is my greatest hope that by hiding the true name, you will not be encouraged to seek the specific place and especially not seek it with any sort of misguided enthusiasm. I am certain there are many other places like it.

Haunted theaters are not all that uncommon and hauntings in general are not uncommon in the south. Though I have not specified whether we are for this story in the south of Virginia, or the south of Wales. I feel it does not matter. The hauntings of each and of many other places are perhaps of equal frequency.

This story begins a long time before I ever set foot in The Consequent, but I cannot begin where I did not start. I have debated, scratched out, deleted, and re-written this beginning many times over. However, with the prodding of Luella and with great faith in God, I am beginning with my foot in the door. I stepped through a frame constructed by the crew, set in half a wall, which was painted to look like bricks and began a tedious monologue of which I only remember one turn of. *The light is oft a harbinger.* It was part of a one act that a local professor had written. We were performing for some esteemed visitors from the school by which it was about to be acquired. Being a friend of another professor, whose theater arts department had yet to fully materialize, I stepped in at his request to give voice to the lead.

The one act was just a small part of the plea. It was merely a jest as the board and committee needed to be impressed upon by the suitableness of our location with a tour of the facility and its given history. The Consequent dates back to the late seventeen hundreds and though small, has been host to a variety of well-known historical figures. It is often believed theaters have the ability to hold the impressions and emotions of those that have been so affected by what they witness during a performance that their excitement, or empathic sorrow seeps from their souls and settles into the fixtures, carpets, and boards. It is often believed that we are pulling back more than a velvet curtain when we open a show, that something we give and something we take will linger long after our words and mimicries have passed. It was on this particular occasion that I began to believe this was true.

Luella had told me for some time now that she could not be alone at the theater. And that she could especially not be alone in the house portion of the building. This was problematic, as Luella owned the theater. She had purchased it as an investment, but was so unsettled by it over time, that within two years of working with the community on her own accord, she was more than willing to give it up to the school when the board came to her later that day and offered what should have been too little of a sum. One of the deans had had a very vivid dream about the place, which he would never elaborate on, but I watched him salivate the moment he came across the threshold for the first time. This man, we will call, Dr. Oren. (As I have mentioned, I do not wish anyone to seek this place out for themselves, and as such, all names have been altered).

Dr. Oren, though he was the author of the one act, had never set foot at The Consequent before his dream and not even before the day they came to tour the theater and decide on details of the acquisition. He had come to the school's physics department only the previous year, so why the board was so eager to promote and listen to this man's strangely eager request is beyond my knowledge. I am told he practically demanded an offer be made and that he had already stalked Luella in an effort to divine what kind of a woman she was and what might have to be done to take the theater from her. I am also told he shrieked when the offer was both made and accepted.

As I stepped through the door, built for the one act, and began my monologue, my eyes wandered to the upper stage right portion of the house, as they often did whether during a performance, or during an after-hours meander. Luella had often told me that was where she saw him. I thought perhaps it was merely where she thought she saw him. I'd been searching for some time to ascertain what poor combination of lighting, shadows, and structure of row might be giving her the impression that there was indeed a man of dark shadow seated and watching. She claimed she always saw him in the third to last row, in the fourth seat from the end, nearest the side aisle and wall. I had never seen anyone sit there, not even during a sold-out performance of Hamlet performed by a popular traveling troupe during which I had purposely sat myself to be in view of the seat for the whole portion of the show. Luella had been seated next to me but shook her head whenever I looked at her with an inquiring glance. I had, however, watched people scoot by, maneuvering as if going around someone, and mouthing apologies, both before the start of the performance and at intermission. Luella had not stayed after intermission. On the night of the one act, she was there, watching me, and thus watching my eyes wander upward and over till my breath caught in my throat and I stumbled over a line. My professor friend gave me an uncomfortable glare, I did not witness (though was later told about by him), yet I doubt it could have been as uncomfortable a notion as that given by Luella when my eyes quickly found their way to hers and she simply nodded in reply.

There he was. I did not wish to believe it, but there he was. Even when I looked away and back. Taking a shock, but also filled with wild elation, I had to try not to grin, or laugh, or throw my hand above my brow to try for a better look while blocking the stage lights. I knew I should be looking at our esteemed visitors with their deeper than deep pockets, but I looked up at the un-empty seat in the third to last row and poured my performance out for him, whoever he was. Even when my monologue ended and I was to be interacting with the other players, I kept directing my focus at him, wanting him to know that I knew he was watching. The other players, of which there were only two, were less than thrilled with my performance. Hiro, being especially put out, wouldn't talk to me immediately afterwards. Like I, he had not believed in such a visitor, or any of the others that we had been informed were inhabiting The Consequent. Hiro was a man of science and art, keeping the two at an arm's length from each other at all times. Callie though—Callie with her crystals strung on a cord and tucked beneath her moss green turtleneck, chastised me lightly. *Told you so,* she had sing-songed, cupping her hands around my face. *Told you so.*

Callie a few months before this, had convinced Luella to allow a medium to visit and conjure an explanation of the man in the third to last row. Luella had not wanted to consult a medium or anyone but being vexed into a curious desire to know who was haunting her theater, had finally caved. Callie was a bit of a medium in training herself but claimed that she wasn't quite skilled enough to procure any sort of information. When the medium arrived, she bolted straight for the stage where she made an exclamation, a yelp so loud that Luella tumbled into a door frame with fright. I saw the bruise on her jawbone the next day when I met her for coffee in hopes of calming her nerves. Only she and Callie had been with the medium and Callie wouldn't stop blowing up Luella's phone with excited texts about that evening's findings. I took the phone and turned on Do Not Disturb mode. Before she put it away, Luella read me some of the texts. It seemed the medium had felt the presence of four entities, only one of which she was certain was a human spirit. She wasn't sure about the child that beckoned her to a game of hide and seek behind the curtains before running off madly giggling down the back hall. And she wasn't sure about the man in the third to last row. Apparently, it was he who caused her outburst that sent Luella into the doorframe. Also, she seemed to believe we had a ghost dog in the sound booth. The one she was certain was a human spirit was the lady in grey. I scoffed, perhaps a little too loudly, when I read that one. How many hauntings have a lady in grey, or a lady in white? It seemed all too contrived. And why on earth would there be a ghost dog in the sound booth?

I soon ordered two black coffees and two slices of hot banana bread. Luella kept staring out the window, not saying much, shaking her head in the direction of the street that leads down to The Consequent, and gingerly tapping her jawbone. When I was halfway through my banana bread, she finally spoke.

"Morely, I don't know about the medium, but I know there is someone who sits up there. And I know that Callie, amongst others, have heard whispers in the wings. Even Hiro has turned his head, as if listening for a cue when he doesn't need one. The sound booth is always cold, except for the floor. The floor stays warm."

"Probably, from the electronics–in the booth," I replied.

She nodded and then shook her head again. "I wish I'd never bought the place."

I was happy for her when a reprieve seemed to arrive with the offer from the school. It would not come, however, without the theater giving us one last show. On the day of the one act and tour, I went into the sound booth for a chat, while Hiro and Luella took the guests through the rest of the building. The two techs, whom I had known for some time, were wearing wool sweaters and flip flops. We made small talk about how they both seemed to be having trouble with their allergies.

"Did you hear me sneeze during your monologue? Sorry about that," said the one we'll call Venti.

"No, I didn't catch it. No worries."

"We're always sneezing in here," he said.

"And freezing," added the one we'll call River.

"What are you allergic to? Wool?" I asked.

"No, pollen and dogs," said River.

"Yeah, we're both allergic to dogs. And I'm allergic to turkey," said Venti.

We all left the booth a moment later, at my behest, suggesting we go outside and take a walk in the afternoon sun. As we got to the doors leading out to the lobby, there was a loud boom from the speakers and "Changes" by David Bowie came blasting through, reverberating the walls at an immense volume. The three of us jumped and snapped our heads around. We said nothing. We side-eyed each other, all knowing that Venti had double-checked the tower was off before we exited the booth. The curtain on stage left rustled and Callie poked her head out from around it.

"What for?" she yelled.

We didn't say anything. She threw her hands in our direction. "Better turn it off fast," she called.

Venti and River headed back to the booth. I remained motionless. For years I had come into this building, performed in this house, and never encountered anything odd. Now, twice in the span of an hour, I had encountered both the man in the third to back row, and the ghost dog of the sound booth, who apparently likes the sounds of David

Bowie. The man I could not explain away, but perhaps this happening with the sound was just an accident, a weird glitch in the electronics.

Venti poked his head out of the booth, his face pale and his eyes wide. "It's off," he said. "The tower is still off. The player is vibrating though."

There was a six- disc CD player in the booth that the crew sometimes used to play music before or after hours when they were working. It was usually loaded with some assortment of what we would call 70's-90's classics.

There was a loud blipping, deflating sound, and the music stopped. River poked her head out. "I kept pushing the power button on the player. Maybe it was stuck?"

"Did it seem stuck?" asked Venti.

River frowned and went back into the booth. A moment later she came back out holding Venti by the elbow and marched him past me on out through the lobby until her face found the glow of the afternoon sun.

We stayed outside until our esteemed visitors left. My professor friend saw us seated on a nearby bench and came over to shake hands and say goodbye. I stood to greet him. Over his shoulder, I watched Dr. Oren eyeball the exterior of The Consequent, still salivating, and now looking like he was in need of the gentlemen's facilities. He shifted his weight back and forth from left to right and front to back. He paced. He beamed feverishly and rubbed his palms together, even throwing them up with fingers outstretched into what are commonly known as jazz hands. In short, he behaved like a giddy, drunken, child.

My friend saw me watching and patted me on the back in a pretense to lean close to my ear and whispered, "Oren's a strange one, isn't' he? I caught him messing with the lights on the stage."

When Venti, River, and I had gone back inside we found the others in the middle of the lobby. I should note here that the lobby is small. The biggest things in the lobby are the windowless doors that go into the house. Aside from those doors there is an entrance to a hall on the left that leads off to the restroom facilities and another entrance to a hall on the right that leads to a small office and to the backstage doors. The walls are cream and the floors are carpeted red. There is a small fountain that used to send water flowing over two stone swans swimming above tiny purple tiles, but it has not worked in a long time. Those details are something that I have written and changed my mind on many times over because I do not wish to give away too many features and thus give away the identity of the theater. These details, however, do come into play with what happens next and if I'm going to tell the whole story, they cannot be left out.

We had found the others in the middle of the lobby. Callie was clearly distraught, and Hiro was doing his best to calm her down. Luella stood very still, mumbling that she was sorry, but it had to be done.

"What has to be done?" asked Venti.

"She sold it to that awful school. We all have to go. She gave away our jobs," Callie said.

Hiro rolled his eyes. "Do you blame her? Calm down. We all have day jobs anyway."

"You do!" she shouted. "You do!" Callie stormed off down the hall to the restrooms.

"She's got a job, doesn't she?" said Venti. "She's a medium in training, or something."

"Not quite a job," said River. "Did you really sell it? Are we really out?"

Luella sighed. "Part of the deal. The school needs the roles to go to students if they're going to have the program they want. I'm sorry. I really need to let this place go."

"Money!" shouted Callie from somewhere down the hall.

"It's not about the money. I just have to let it go," said Luella.

I gave her my best empathetic smile and told her that I was happy for her and declared that we should all be happy for her. The school was to take acquisition in two days. Other than our one act, there hadn't been a show for a few weeks, so there wasn't much to do other than to make sure our personal items were not left behind. Luella would lock up that evening and we would say our goodbyes to The Consequent. She and Hiro tried to impress upon the others that they could always come back as guests and simply enjoy whatever the students had to offer. It would be different, but enjoyable, and not so much a permanent goodbye. It would be a *see you later*. Besides, it was a small town, and we would all keep in touch and gather together now and then.

I shared in these sentiments. It wasn't that I didn't care for the place, because I did care for it very much. It simply occurred to me that perhaps the place had been saying good-bye, as if it, or they, knew that it was our last evening, and the one act had been our last performance for them. The shadowed man had allowed me to view him, and the sound booth dog had played us a song it understood. As these thoughts ran comfortingly along, out of the corner of my eye, I spotted something glint across the house doors. It shimmered like sunlight yet was cold in appearance as if moonlight. I turned my head and would have thought nothing of it, except Callie having returned from the restroom had stopped short upon re-entering the lobby and was staring at the doors. We exchanged apprehensive glances. I got to the doors first, pushed through them and found all the house lights to be off.

"Hey Luella, did you already turn the lights out?" I called.

"No," she replied. Then she was at my back, peering in. "Who turned them off?" she called to the others.

No one replied and we knew that it hadn't been us, but still, it perhaps could have been our guests. Except Luella, as if reading my thoughts, said that our guests had all exited as a group without having gone back into the house after the performance. This meant that Venti,

River, and I had been the last ones in there. Callie came dancing in beside us. She walked to the back row and put her hands on a couple of the seat backs.

"Can we have the lights back on?" she called out. "So, we can say good-bye?"

There was a moment of silence and then I could have sworn I heard the shuffle of the CD player clicking around its carousel of discs, but that seemed like an odd thing to hear from just inside the doorway, from away and outside the booth. Then the lights came on. At first just the center stage light beamed down, which as anyone who has worked in theater knows, is controlled separately from the house lights. The house lights came on next. They were dim at first but then raised to the brightest they could go. We collectively looked toward the dimmer switch on the wall and saw that it was pushed all the way up. I looked over my shoulder to see if Venti and River had joined us, but they were still in the lobby, sitting on the fountain ledge and looking at the floor.

No sooner had I glanced back than the door swung forcefully at Luella, who was still holding it open with her foot, knocking her back into the lobby. The door immediately swung back, closed. I pushed the door to open it, to make sure she was okay, but the door stuck fast. These doors were not doors that stuck. They were always loose. They never even creaked. They just swung, except now they were stuck. I tried them both. Luella was saying something from the other side. I think it was my name.

The fog of my mind came fast and heavy. I could just barely make out the shape of Callie moving down the center aisle. She twirled, arms up in a ballerina pose, but wrong. She was normally a graceful woman, but in this forming cloud she seemed clumsy and the only word that I could truly think to describe her movement was whirligig. She was whirligigging down the aisle.

The floor was moving. I was pretty sure of that. I made my way toward the sound booth with great difficulty, as if I were fighting against a conveyor belt that was moving in the opposite direction of where I needed to go. I remember hoping that Venti or River had left their cell phone inside of the booth. I'm not sure who I thought I was going to call. A medic? Luella? The fire department? We did call them later—the fire department. The sound booth door was shut and would not open. This did not surprise me in the least and while I normally would have been taken aback at what accompanied its closure, it did not phase me when there came a whimpering and a scratching from the other side of the door. I did surprise myself by kneeling and leaning with my back against the door and saying, "It's alright. There now. It's okay, old friend—just changes."

The whimpering and scratching stopped. There was a thump against the lower part of the door where I was leaning, as if a dog had pressed its weight against the door and settled down.

"It's going to be okay," I said. Though, I am not sure if I said it for the supposed dog, or for myself.

"Do you hear her?" shouted Callie. "Can you hear her?" Peering around the exterior corner of the booth, I saw that she had made her way onto the ledge of the orchestra pit. She was balancing at an odd angle like a tightrope walker on a warped spring.

"Do you hear her? She's singing! She's singing! Something like Haydn or Bach!" she called out.

I heard nothing other than the heaviness of the air, if you can really call it a sound at all. It was as if everything and nothing were in my ears all at once. I glanced to my right and there in the third to last row, fourth seat from the end, nearest the side aisle was the shadowed man. I could see him more clearly now than when I had been on stage. Shadowed didn't really do justice to his features. He was deeply dark, opaque, the kind of dark that I can only compare to being in a cave when taken on a tour and the guide turns out all the lights to give you an idea of what true darkness looks like. He was that kind of dark, maybe darker. There were no features, just a sense of shape. He was watching Callie, or at least looking in her direction, but I had the distinct feeling that he was watching her. His head shape tilted and then turned toward me. I saw no face, but I knew that our eye shapes were locked. For every bit of menace that I anticipated would be hurled at me, I felt nothing but mild fear of what I did not comprehend. Perhaps he too was attempting to comprehend me. Perhaps he too felt a mild fear. He rose from his seat, arm shapes pushing up, hip shapes bending and straightening. He exited into the side aisle and shaped against the wall so that he appeared to be climbing it and wafted into the recess of a corner where I found I could no longer detect him. I would not be truly afraid until that night, when lying in bed alone my mind would regain enough presence to start deciphering what I had experienced. I have heard the same from others who have stories like mine. It is very hard for the mind to fear what it cannot comprehend.

"Take care little one." I gently pushed my hand against the sound booth door before I stood up. "Callie, it's time to go," I called out to her. I walked around the booth into the center aisle and found her staring down into the orchestra pit. Her mood had shifted. The house had continued shifting and my feet still moved against a backward conveyor. Her mood was backwards too. She frowned into the pit.

"He jumped in there. She was singing so loud, and he jumped right onto the piano. He wants me to come down and play. Not music, just play. It's just too loud up here."

"Callie, it's time to go," I called.

"I don't want to go, but I don't think I should play," she said.

The house swung sideways. The stage left seating was entirely on the wall. The side aisle was on the ceiling, and I still upon the center aisle had moved to where the stage left seating had been. The orchestra pit was a straight shot ahead of me.

"Callie, we need to go now."

"He's so persistent. He's so—so very..." She wobbled, arms waving in erratic ways that made no sense. She lifted her left foot to slide down toward the floor, away from the pit, but in the madness of it all her left foot went over her head and her right foot slid toward the floor. She landed with the thud of her stomach on the ledge. I expected the wind to be knocked out of her lungs, but it escaped with a scream so horrendous I will never be able to wipe it from my mind. I was halfway down the aisle, the carpet rolling up toward my ankles, my feet leaping over the waves. I was running to grab her, and she was flinging backwards and falling toward me. We scrambled to each other as the house swung again. The stage right audience seats blocked our exit. Hand in hand we jumped, and I cannot tell you how, but we leapt upward and hovered and fled, row, over row to the right-side lobby doors that were now all the way to the left. We fell upon them and much to our relief they opened.

Not to our relief was an empty lobby. The floor was cream, and the walls were carpeted red. Tiny sparks as if from a festive sparkler flew from the top of the fountain, which was now mounted on the wall. The purple tiles dripped over the swan's wings. We called out to the others, but they did not answer. Barreling for the doors, we burst out into a setting blaze of sunlight, pink skies, and deep violet clouds silhouetting Hiro on the sidewalk.

"Call the fire department," Callie was screaming. I thought she meant it for the fountain on the wall. "The piano in the pit is on fire. The child is down there. But he's not. He's not!"

"He's not what?" Hiro grabbed her shoulders and tried to steady her with his eyes.

"What child?" called out Venti who came running from the side alley of the theater.

"He's not a child!" Callie collapsed into Hiro's arms. Hiro stood holding her the way one might hold an alligator.

"Luella? River?" I ran to Venti.

"They're out back. We were trying to break in a window. The backstage doors wouldn't budge from the inside. We were trying to get

27

you guys out. Did you hear the singing?" He pulled his phone from his pocket and before I could reply, he was speaking with emergency services, requesting help for a fire. I took off down the alley, skidding on gravel.

When the firetrucks arrived, we had all assembled out front. Luella gripped my hand and would not let go, leading me with her to speak to the fire crew, tagging along with me when I spoke to the chief separately. It wasn't until I dropped her off at her townhouse two miles away that she finally let go of my hand. The fire crew had not found a fire. They had found a shabby old theater with cream walls, red carpet, and nice big windowless doors that swung freely into the house. There was nothing in the pit, except an old, four-pedal piano unmarked by anything but time.

River had relieved Hiro of Callie. She took Callie home, made her some tea, and at Callie's request helped her to remove all the crystals from her jewelry box and nightstand and rehome them into a junk drawer. She had wanted them out of sight but not entirely gone. Venti later told me River expressed a bit of remorse over this when two weeks later they were out shopping downtown and ran into Callie, wearing one of the larger crystals on a rope around her neck.

As for The Consequent, it stands looking the same as it ever has. Rumors come out every now and again about certain happenings during performance nights, or when students are working late and alone. Dr. Oren feverishly visits the theater every day and has taken to playing the piano. My professor friend claims Dr. Oren has never had a lesson but plays beautifully as if he had been a prodigy.

Many times, in the writing of this story, the shape of something has lingered at the base of the wall. I see it not just with the corners of my eyes, but when I look straight on. The words are often backtracked as the backspace key descends without my pressing. I am concerned that by the time this reaches you it may be missing pieces or present itself with additions that I am unaware of. However it reaches you, Luella and I sincerely hope your treading into old theaters comes with an awareness and delicacy of what lies within.

Chapter 2

November 30, 2022

In the pocket of her purse there was a long, folded sheet of paper. In purple ink on yellow paper, Franley Parker kept her records secret. She did not share them with anyone, except for her husband. She never felt that anyone would understand, nor was she sure that she understood. In fact, she was certain that she did not. Bill, her husband, did not understand either, but he did not mock her. Franley's hope in the record keeping was that a reason may emerge in some pattern, quality, or information that when looked at in the light of reasoning would give way to a cause and an understanding for them both.

She had been keeping this record for about four years. The facts within dated back further and some things that were facts had been left out and not written down anywhere. Those left out things she referred to as the Outliers and she referred to them only in her subconscious because not only were they too strange to be recorded, they were too unsettling to be summoned to the front of her mind. They were left to waft at the periphery and readily be shoved away should they attempt to step into the light.

Smoothing the top flap of her faux red leather purse, and shifting her weight in her black, round-toed boots, Franley attempted to soothe her nerves and secure a firm posture before pressing the doorbell adjacent to the sullen door of the brownstone before which, she now stood. First encounters were always awkward and especially would be today, given that her purpose here was disguised by another. Once pressed, the bell chimed a whimsical tune that was familiar, but not readily nameable. Two moments later the sullen door opened, and a warm, ruddy face beamed out at her.

"Hello, hello!" the face called out as the man attached to it pulled the door back and gestured for her to come in.

"Hi. Mortimer Blackwood?" Franley asked to be sure.

"Indeed," he replied. "Franley Parker?"

"Indeed," she nodded, stepping in.

Mortimer did a quick sweep of the yard with his eyes before pulling the door behind them.

"May I take your jacket?" he asked, motioning from the hall tree to her black denim.

"No, thank you though. I can't stay long. I don't want to take up much of your time."

"I wouldn't mind if you did, to be honest. Being retired isn't all it's cracked up to be. It gets a little boring around here most days." He smiled at her and walked past into the sitting room that was cozily just inside the front door.

There was a wood fire burning. Cream painted walls were set nicely against the warm exposed brick surrounding the hearth. *Cozy. Inviting. Welcoming.* The words tumbled around in her mind. A realtor is always labeling rooms and spinning their best qualities. It was an ingrained habit that Franley was sure she would never be able to break.

"Please, sit anywhere you like. Would you like some tea, or a soda?" Mortimer hovered near a doorframe adjacent to a small galley kitchen. His sweater and slacks matched the atmosphere of his home.

Franley wavered a moment longer than she had intended because she had intended on saying no, but with his assurance that it was no trouble and that the water was already boiled, she thanked him for a cup of Earl Grey and then found herself agreeing that a bit of chai seasoning would be nice. It was a grey and cold sort of day with the wind and low cloud coverage and all. And this was nice. *Cozy and inviting and welcoming.* The atmosphere of the home suited not only the attire, but also the demeanor of the host. She wondered if the atmosphere of her home suited her. *Neutrals. Modern. Well kept.* She smoothed down the pockets of her knee length, burnt orange skirt.

"So, they're selling the theater again, are they?" Mortimer queried, handing her the cup of tea. She had chosen a plush green wingback by the fire, and he sat himself in an identical one opposite her.

"They are. I'm not entirely sure why the school has decided to part ways with it, but they have. It's a beautiful building. Maybe a little small for a university of their size and standing? I think they may go back to using the one on campus like they used to. The town is about a twenty-minute hike for them." Franley held the teacup close to her mouth but didn't yet take a sip. She let the steam warm her face and the smell of chai stirred happy memories within.

Mortimer nodded. "Doesn't feel like it's been that long, but I guess it's been a good twenty years since they bought it."

"It has been twenty-one years according to the records. I had heard you might be interested in buying. Have you given it any thought? Dugan told me how Louisa didn't want to let it go." She took a sip of her tea and watched as Mortimer's eyes narrowed over his cup.

"He did? Well, that's sort of a surprise. He never seemed to care much for Louisa's feelings on anything." He sighed and turned to face the hearth. "We're not interested. I don't want it, and Louisa doesn't either. Besides, she is much happier running her store on Main. And I'm pretty sure you could have had that answered over the phone." He turned his face toward her. "I'm sorry if that sounded harsher than I meant for it to. I guess Dugan still gets under my skin. Besides, I knew you were coming here for other reasons." His voice softened at the end.

Franley shifted her weight in the chair and swallowed tea that was still too hot to go down properly. Perhaps it was the hearth, or the chai, or the knowing that she saw in his eyes, for whatever reason, she

33

decided without deciding, simply the words just came out–that it was true, she had come for other reasons.

"How did you know?" she asked, smoothing the top flap of her purse that lay across her knees.

"A friend told me. I don't exactly approve of her methods, but she called me to say that you would be coming by for reasons of your own interest, reasons that I would be familiar with."

"Do I know her? Is she stalking me?" Franley sat up a little straighter, the purse almost falling on the floor.

"No, no, nothing like that," Mortimer laughed. "She's a bit of a sensitive, more so than most."

The way he said sensitive didn't need to be explained to Franley. She knew exactly what he meant. His friend foresaw or knew some way that Franley would be coming here. And she knew that Franley would want to talk about things worthy of purple ink on yellow paper in the pocket of her purse.

"Do you typically have concerns about people stalking you?" Mortimer asked.

"No," Franley blushed. "I just wasn't anticipating anyone unfamiliar with me to know what I was about." She appreciated the smile that moved his fluffy gray eyebrows up in pretend surprise.

"Well, like I said, she's a friend and one familiar with the theater. She was there when the university made the offer to buy it from Louisa. She took it pretty hard when Louisa accepted, but she soon agreed it was the right decision. We had sort of a shared experience."

"Your friend, is her name something akin to Callie?" Franley subconsciously tucked a curl of red hair behind her ear and consciously watched for a reaction.

Mortimer smiled, his eyebrows moved up and down again. "Alicia. But, yes, she is Callie just the same. I thought perhaps you may have read my account. How long have you been a subscriber?"

It was Franley's turn to smile. "You inspired me. I found Imagine Shadows Magazine when I was researching. Now, I'm December 12, 2020. Written a little differently, talking about myself in the third, but true all the same."

"Take a peek around the corner into the kitchen there and tell me what you see on the far wall." Mortimer gestured to the doorway into the kitchen.

Franley leaned over in her chair and squinted. "A bookshelf?"

"Yes, now go take a closer look," he replied.

Franley got up with her teacup, left her purse on the chair, smoothed out her skirt, and went into the kitchen making mental notes about the oak cabinets and the updated appliances. The bookshelf, not to her surprise, contained rows of Imagine Shadows Magazine dating back to 2012 and current up to the last issue. On the second shelf down from the top, she located December 2020 and carried it back to the front room where she handed it over to Mortimer.

"December twelfth," she said. The issues were divided into multiple stories, one for each Saturday of the month, with other filler and hypothetical articles in-between.

"I thought maybe so," he said, taking the magazine from her hand. "There are several realtor stories spread throughout the issues, but I had a hunch this one was you."

"How's that?" she asked, returning to her seat and smoothing the flap of her purse once it was back on her lap.

"Historical building and your fixation with where you are keeping your secrets." He nodded to her purse.

"I guess I have a tell," she replied, looking down at the purse.

Mortimer flipped the pages until he came to Franley's story. He perused it over again, nodding and lifting his brows, occasionally looking up at her over the pages, waxing curious thoughts.

Chapter 3

Imagine Shadows Magazine
   December 12, 2020
   Pocket
   by Ripley Parks
The oven had beeped twice this morning. It wasn't on. She had checked multiple times. It had not been used in two days. Last night they ordered pizza. The night before that they microwaved leftover turkey and potatoes. Jorge made the kids laugh with his potato beard. She made them squirt cold tea from their mouths when she gave Jorge the snarl face. That's what the kids called it. Snarl face was the silly expression Ripley often gave in response to something ridiculously awkward, or funny they had done. It was an, *I see you and you think you're getting at me, but I'm too patient and ridiculous myself. Therefore, it is of no matter because—I love you.* On the surface, it usually meant she was moving on to the next thing and the ridiculousness would temporarily cease.

She eyed the oven and took note of the time on the display. "Time to take a drive, Ripley Parks."

Ripley spoke aloud to herself often. Laughed to herself often. Was alone, often. She grabbed her purse and phone from the kitchen table and headed for the front door. As she was putting the key in the lock, she was sure the oven gave one solitary beep good-bye. It wasn't exactly faint, but a garbage truck inopportunely rolled past at the same moment. *We won't count that one,* she thought. *We won't count it, if we can't be certain of it.* She ran her fingers across the pocket on her skirt. She liked this skirt because it was a favored burnt orange and had deep, flat pockets. It hit professionally just above the knees and wasn't a nuisance when driving. She spent a lot of time driving. Selling older properties often required driving thirty-forty minutes from the busy suburban area they lived in. Historical homes were her favorite. She would sell new construction sometimes, but she didn't really care as much for it. She wasn't particularly good at remembering historical facts, but she loved the charm and warm draw of things past. She loved the smell of a place one hundred years old in the way some women love the smell of men's deodorant. For Ripley, it was the most enticing cologne on the planet.

Today's home was 422 Pin Row Street, originally a post office built in 1939. The current tenants had bought the place about ten years back and remodeled it into a stellar home by modern standards. Ripley could only imagine how depressing it must be to part ways with it. The couple had retired and desired warmer weather out west.

The all-brick postal home possessed about twenty-five hundred square feet of living space, which included a cozy basement of brick walls and bamboo floors. It was a contrast of old versus new, but cozy because it smelled like sweet cigars. This was Ripley's second favorite scent. Some cigars have an awful, gaseous odor, but the basement was filled with the aroma of leathery, cedar goodness. The bricks held all those employed memories of cigar lightings through the decades. There wasn't a clear record of what went where in the original state of the building, so perhaps it had been an employee lounge at some point. The post office had been a small-town post, much smaller than most remaining post offices in the country from that era.

Sadly for Ripley, not a lot was left of the original trappings. The basement bricks, the floors downstairs, a few things here and there throughout, and a concrete slab above the entryway doors imprinted with the words, POST OFFICE. The letters looked proud to be facing outward and onward through time.

The face of the house bore two tall, elongated windows, one on each side with white painted frames. The porch featured slender white columns flanking the front double doors with iron wrapped porch lights to polish the welcome. The original entry had been a single door, and it must have been rather large because they had not altered the door frame width when installing the new ones. The new doors were solid ash alder, charmed with frosted dandelion yellow glass that was inset in square windows. Ripley thought it was a shame that the original door was gone but understood all too well that not everything from the past can be salvaged. The frosted glass was lovely though. It made for excellent curb appeal and an inviting entryway with the warm golden light blanketing the floors across the front half of the downstairs.

Ripley had already met with and listed with the west bound couple. There was to be a showing tomorrow with the clients of another agent. The couple had taken a few days to head out looking for their retirement property. Ripley wanted to make sure the place was still as spectacularly spotless as it had been when she had first taken them on. The lockbox was already set up, so that she and other agents could gain entry while the couple was away.

Ripley parked in the gravel drive and crunched her way up to the front stoop. Admiring the dandelion glass, Ripley fiddled with the lockbox and let herself in. Buttery sunlight streamed and stretched out a welcome as she gently swung the door open.

"Hello. Hello," she said. "It's just me." The postal house answered with silence and somewhere down the street a leaf blower revved up.

In the entryway, with the door shut behind her, Ripley glanced around the living room. The main living room was off to the left with its deep blue sofa postured next to a brick fireplace. The fireplace had been painted white, blanched by current trends. It always bothered

Ripley that people liked to go about painting old fireplaces. She much preferred the shades of red and brown. They were cozier and homier. She had asked the couple to consider putting their television (it had sat in a corner opposite the sofa) away in storage. They had abided and in place of the television was a tall potted plant. The walls in this room were soft yellow, while the rest of the house wore a parchment white.

Off to the right was a sitting area with pastel pink chairs and a coat closet. Straight ahead was a small hall containing the stairs, both for going up to the second floor and for going down to the basement. At the end of the hall sat an eat-in kitchen and adjacent was the entry to the office. Though Ripley was left to daydream of gilded post-boxed walls, this office at the back of the house was practically untouched except for new furnishings. It stood to remind the occupants of its former glory.

The door to the office was the original. It was a wooden door bearing white frosted glass and the words POSTMASTER painted in black. It made Ripley giddy whenever she saw it. Its black metal doorknob had once been turned by this POSTMASTER and his employees. Though the desk she imagined him sitting at was long gone, the office held other delights. It was filled with books on cases that reached from floor to ceiling. The sellers had outfitted the room with two leather wingbacks and a red rug that lay in between them. There were two windows and a large ink stain under the back one that looked out into a sizeable yard. The other window, straight across from the door, looked out toward the neighbors. One could just make out another house through some brambles, hedges, and a small alleyway. Ripley liked this room most.

Things seemed in order at the front of the house, so she headed straight for the back. The upstairs with its two bedrooms and oversized full bath, could wait. As she neared the end of the hall, Ripley heard the slightest creak of a door. She glanced into the kitchen, eyeing the back door. It seemed closed, but she walked over and gave it a push to be sure. She surveyed the room. The kitchen appeared orderly with its granite countertops and chopping block island. She thought the granite was a precocious addition. It would help sell the home because everyone loves granite countertops, but that didn't seem as important as preserving character.

The dining table and chairs were neat and tidy and painted black. They matched the doorknob to the office, which was just a few feet past them with the door ajar. Ripley stood very still for a moment. She had hurried out of the hall and into the kitchen without even glancing toward that room. Perhaps that was a mistake. Perhaps someone was in the office.

Do you really believe someone is in there? She silently asked herself.

No. She silently replied. *No, I do not.*

Ripley made a snarl face and walked to the office door.

"Postmaster," she said, "I'm rather in love with your office."

She gave a little knock on the door and then pushed it open. The lowering of the winter sun was shining in from the window across from the door. Shadows lay on the red rug and played at the feet of the wingback chairs. The ink stain sat like its own constant shadow under the back window. Sighing, she ran her fingers across her skirt pocket. It made a slight crinkling sound.

"Well, you are perfect." She smiled at the room. The bookshelves spanned both walls that were without windows. The ceiling was only nine feet high, but floor to ceiling books were always an impressive sight. She felt as though the room was smiling back.

"Books to my left. Books to my right. Oh Books, what a beautiful sight." Ripley sang this ditty to herself and laughed to herself. She often sang to herself, or to her children. Little made up things. Little bits of nonsense. Sometimes they laughed too.

"Oh, but you—you over here. You are what I'm really interested in."

Ripley approached the ink stain and knelt down. She ran her fingers delicately across history. It was about the size of a plate that would accompany a teacup. *What would one call that? A tea plate? Sounds messy.*

She giggled and blushed, finding she was suddenly embarrassed, though she could not say exactly why. There wasn't anyone listening or watching. There wasn't anyone to think her ridiculous. *And isn't that why I like you so much, ink blot? Let's not call you a stain. Just a past that can't look at me. Oh, but I can look at you.*

"Well, I will sit with you for a moment anyway. Then I have to check on the rest of the place." Ripley took her hand away from the ink stain and settled onto the floor with her knees to the side and her legs curling back around her. She stared fondly at the ink. She looked the part of a far away dreamer and also a little sad.

Ripley could not say how long she had sat there. She had been far away. Down the inkwell. Speaking with the POSTMASTER. Asking for a job. She sorted mail from all over the world. She handled the places that it came from. She left her fingerprints on the places it was going. It was true that in this post office, much of the mail had been local and not very much global, until the Second World War. There had been a lot of global mail then. This reminded her of something, and that memory pulled her from the inkwell in the floor and back into the shadows of nightfall. She gave the ink stain a gentle caress and pushed herself up onto her feet. Smoothing her skirt and patting the pocket, she took note of the dark and wondered at the time. She found a light switch by the door and flipped it. The overhead beamed on. In the soft yellow glow, Ripley turned to the bookshelf directly before her and ran her fingers across the fourth row of books from the bottom.

"Here we go," she said, pulling a green bound encyclopedia of birds from the shelf. She flipped open the book.

The pages fell away from the middle, exactly as she had intended they would. '*Mourning Dove.*' Pressed therein, against the sketch of a grayish bird, lay a sheet of purple three cent stamps. The stamps featured a white eagle with his wings up stretched into a V shape. He held arrows in his talons and the words, 'Win the War,' were printed across his chest. The husband of the westbound couple had shown her the stamps when she first came to see the house. He had found them in the basement when the remodel work was being done. They were in excellent shape. They looked as if they had just arrived freshly printed.

"Pocket."

Ripley jumped and whipped her head around. She heard it, distinctly. *Pocket*. Someone said *Pocket*. The doorway was empty, as was the room with the exception of herself. She touched her fingers to her skirt pocket, eyes darting about, heart pounding. Slowly, she looked back at the stamps and cautiously closed the encyclopedia. She wished the stamps had been framed and displayed on the wall. They would give echo to the history of the place, and one wouldn't have to worry about bending their edges inside of a book.

"I really need more sleep," she said. Resolving to get her things and go, she put a hand to her shoulder, then glanced down at the floor and all around the room.

"In the car. I left my purse in the car." Ripley pushed her hand over her pocket.

My phone. They're going to be worried. And mad. I have no idea, the time. Ripley Parks you are the worst.

"Pocket."

Ripley Parks froze. Pin needles and cold whispers of air went down her back.

The voice had been right there, right in her ear. A man's voice. A soft voice. There wasn't an unkindness to it, but disembodied voices were not exactly her favorite. Ripley had her back to the bookshelf, facing the ink stain. Strangely, the ink was growing. It was slow, but yes, it was spreading out. The radius of the tea plate sized stain was expanding. Now it was a dinner plate. Ripley broke her gaze and bolted for the door. She flipped the light switch down as she flew out of the room. *Realtor habits.* She immediately wished that she had not. Everything should be dark, but it wasn't. Turning the corner into the hall, there was a light coming from the basement. The stairwell was lit from below. There was no light fixture in the stairwell and there was a door at the bottom that was always kept shut. The drafty basement with its lovely cigar smells could easily chill the house above. There was one large fluorescent overhead within. If there was a light coming up the stairwell, the door had to be open.

Here in the nightfall darkened house alone, the only light to be seen was coming up from an unoccupied room. The smell of cigars lightly filtered through. It was lovely, but not now. Not now. Most people are afraid of the dark, but Ripley found she was very afraid of this light. It was unnatural. She wasn't even sure it was light from the overhead. It seemed to sway, and the basement fluorescent was bolted in one long rectangular set of tubes. This light swayed like a hand waving to her. *Come here. Come now. Come see.* That drawing motion of one eager to pull close another, beckoned. Light to shadow. Light to shadow. *Come now. Please. I desire to tell you. I need you.* It swayed like a chandelier, like a lantern rocking on the back of a carriage. Dancing. Galloping.

Ripley pulled herself from the enchantment and fled for the front doors. She flung one open and as she did so, there was a loud bang. The swaying light went out. Her heart leapt into her eye sockets, and she echoed the bang with the slam of the door. She frantically fumbled down the stoop, kicking over the lockbox on her way. She prayed the car would be unlocked.

Fortunately, it was.

Twelve missed calls. *Twelve.* The phone was sitting in the cup holder and plugged into the USB. She would call them on the way via voice command. The car hummed and the gravel crunched as she began to back out of the driveway. The house sat silent and dark. The concrete

POST OFFICE shone in the headlights. And she knew without a doubt that if she re-entered the house this very moment, the lights would remain off.

Everything would be in order. There would be no voice and no occupants in the basement. This is the way things went for Ripley. She could walk down to that basement, and nothing would be waiting for her. Nothing but the lovely smell of cigars.

Still, she always ran away.

She gave the voice command, "Call home." She put the car in drive and pulled forward. The gravel crunching slowed. She put the car in park and waited two rings for an answer.

"Hey, Ripley." The voice of Jorge came over the speakers.

"Jorge, I'm sorry. I know I'm late. Real late," Ripley spoke.

There was silence for a moment.

"We were worried Ripley. I pick the kids up–fine. Pick up dinner–fine. Sun goes down–no mom. Eight o'clock—no mom. Nine o'clock—no mom. Not fine Ripley." His voice was patient but deeply bothered. "Where are you?"

"I'm at the post office house. I got distracted," she replied.

"Does this have anything to do with your list?" he asked.

She wished that he hadn't. "List?"

"You left it in your jeans pocket. It fell out when I went to do laundry," he said.

"I guess that's why it was on the nightstand this morning." She had not remembered leaving it there, but there it had been when she woke up. She had blamed it on forgetfulness and maybe other things and then folded it neatly into her skirt pocket when she got dressed. Perhaps she should start keeping it elsewhere, so that it did not end up in the laundry again.

"You need to come home Ripley."

"I was going to."

"Going to? Ripley—"

"I will. I just—I—win the war," she blurted.

"What? Ripley, come on."

"Jorge, I'll be home. Kiss the kids. Please. I'm so sorry. I love you." And then she hung up.

She knew she needed to go home. They needed her to go home. Still, she couldn't go, not yet. She ran her fingers across her pocket before slipping them inside and pulling out the folded paper.

August 4, 2018

Cotton Farmhouse - a glass fell from a closed kitchen cabinet and broke. No one was in the kitchen. The glass had been at the back of the cabinet, behind some bowls.

August 12, 2018

Cotton Farmhouse - final walk through with buyers. Living room sofa pillows were found on the floor. They were on the sofa when we went upstairs. They were on the floor when we came back down.

October 7, 2018

1950s Ranch - The back bedroom made me ill. I threw up. Gave the listing to Ada.

October 29, 2018

Bar House - loud sounds of glass clinking in empty dining room. I was alone and opening the drapes in the front room.

November 3, 2018

Bar House - shuffling sounds and a thump upstairs. Sellers heard it too. They said they had never heard anything like that before. I mentioned the glasses. They seemed surprised. No laws here against selling - what? A haunted house? They are calling someone to check for raccoons.

November 14, 2018

Sold the Bar House - smoke detector in my home attic goes off. There's no smoke. It's freezing up there. Needs batteries, I guess.

December 5, 2018

Home - attic smoke detector goes off again. No smoke. I replaced the batteries back in November. Jorge brought home a new one today.

THE CONSEQUENT

December 7, 2018

Home - came home around noon and the attic smoke detector was going off. The brand new one. I took it down and removed the batteries. I did not put new ones in. I stared at the empty battery compartment for five solid minutes before I turned to walk away. It did not beep, but flashed its tiny red light repeatedly, as I was walking away. I gave it a snarl face.

December 21, 2018

New Construction - tapped on shoulder while talking with client. There were only three of us. The party of two clients standing in front of me - mother/daughter pair and myself. I turned around and there was no one. Shrugged it off. Made them laugh.

December 22, 2018

New Construction – tapped on should while talking with another client. This time the tapping was repeated in sets of five taps. Over and over. Until the client left. I heard someone whisper, "thank you," when standing alone in the front room.

January 2, 2019

Post Office House - porch lights flipped on and off when the sellers and I left at the same time. Both of us were in our separate cars. They didn't seem to notice.

This was a short list in purple ink on yellow paper. Ripley had been subjected to these types of events for most of her life. She had never spoken openly about them and only in recent months had begun to write them down. She had not shared the list with anyone. Now, Jorge knew. That would be quite the conversation to look forward to. Ripley wasn't truly worried. He had put up with her other quirks. He was far too generous in general; at least she knew he was far more generous than she. She had never done laundry before the rest of the house was awake. He did things like that all the time. Their children were generous too. They would forgive her for being gone tonight. They would greet her with a surplus of hugs and kisses in the morning.

She turned off the car and got out. The headlights of the car stayed on for a moment. As she made her way to the door, Ripley folded the list and slid it back in place.

"What do you care about my pocket?" she whispered.

The night was cold, and the house was colder. There was no light to be seen when she re-entered and shut the door behind her. Briefly the headlights shone in through the dandelion windows, but they faded out. She heard a car speed past with its bass blaring. It was gone in two seconds and there was only silence in the dark.

"I'm done running now," Ripley spoke into the air.

She flipped on the switch for the porch lights. Now she would be a little more prepared if she had to make a fast exit. Ripley waited a moment then began to walk down the hall. She kept the inside lights off. It would be easier to watch for the unexpected, unnatural ones.

Her footsteps on the hard floor remained the only sound. *What are you doing Ripley?* As this thought entered her mind there was a shift of weight on the floor behind her with a soft muffle.

She stopped and waited.

"Pocket?" asked Ripley.

There was a moment of nothing then with a heavy force, Ripley was shoved aside and into the wall. Something rushed past and a rain of thuds clamored down the stairs to the basement. She could hear the door trembling, as if it were at war with itself. Trying to tug itself open. Trying very hard to stay shut.

Ripley ran to the stairwell. She reached the top as the door at the bottom flew open and the swaying light burst out. The swinging, beckoning light that had called her before was calling her again. She really had not expected this. She had thought there would be nothing. There should be nothing, but lovely cigar smells and bricks and fluorescent tubes fastened to the ceiling. Yes, she was done running, but still she thought there would be nothing, not tonight.

She stepped down onto the top step.

"NO."

The voice was very loud. The door to the POSTMASTER's office creaked. Ripley stepped back into the hall. The swaying of the light increased. *Now. Now. Come now!* She ran for the POSTMASTER. The light flaying shadows on the walls as she ran. She took the corner hard and slammed into the partially open door. Grabbing the black knob, she pushed the door shut and pressed against it. She was muttering prayers and trying to regain control of her breathing that had grown frantic. There was a keyhole on the door, but of course she had no key. Through the frosted glass, she could see that the light had gone out. She was in the dark again, but she knew she was not alone.

With two deep breaths, Ripley stepped away from the door. The fact that she was running from something terrible, being helped by a disembodied voice, and now in dire need of a skeleton key, was not lost on her. She began to laugh. She bent her hands to her knees and laughed. She stumbled across the room laughing and slouched down by the ink stain, which was back to its normal size. Taking a deep breath, she leaned back, putting her head against the windowsill.

"I guess a locked door wouldn't really help much anyway," she said to whomever might be listening.

Though there was no moon, a little light from the outside world came in through the windows. Ripley ran her hands over the ink and kept an eye on the door. A slight movement came from the bookshelf where the stamps were hidden. One of the books was sliding forward. It fell to the floor. Another one gradually did the same. Like lemmings, the books one by one began to flee the shelves and drop to the floor. The bottom row looked rather ridiculous as they only had a little hop to make. The top row by the ceiling made the most dramatic tumble. One by one, they all fell down, except for the green encyclopedia of birds. It could no longer stay upright because its friends on either side had left the nest. It fell over flat but remained on the shelf. High on adrenaline, Ripley watched this display with amusement.

"You've made a bit of a mess. If you wanted me to see the stamps again, you could have just pulled that one off." She was still keeping an eye on the door.

"What do you want me to do?" she asked.

"Pocket," came the man's voice.

Ripley got up. She ran her fingers across her skirt pocket.

"Pocket," came the voice again. The bird encyclopedia began to slide from one end of its shelf to the other. Back and forth. Back and forth.

"Pocket," he said.

Ripley walked up to the pile of books on the floor. She reached out for the encyclopedia. It flew from the shelf and slammed into the wall across the room. The stamps slid out at an angle.

"What the—what—what was that for!" she exclaimed. It was then with the shelves entirely empty that she noticed the shelves were not part of one large bookcase. She could see clearly that there were four, floor to ceiling cases. There was a slight gap between the two cases that met in the middle and that gap also extended floor to ceiling. She pushed the discarded books out of the way, making a path to the shelves. She put her fingers up to the gap and pulled to the right. The case did not move. She pulled harder, with her full weight this time. Still, nothing happened. Taking a step back, Ripley looked down at the floor and saw the trace of an indention, or possibly a track beneath the case.

Leaning against the case, she gave it one hard shove and the whole tall thing slid backward. She pulled it to the right once more and the case slid behind the case next to it. She pushed the other center case to the back and to the left and it slid behind the case on the other end.

"Pocket," she said. "Pocket doors."

She had seen pocket doors plenty of times, but she had never seen pocket door bookcases.

"This is just the thing I've always wanted to find," she said, staring out into a small room that was hidden behind the wall of the hallway and behind the sitting room at the front of the house, the one with the pastel pink chairs.

She had not forgotten about the dangerously swaying light, or being shoved by an unseen force, but for the moment she did not care. Ripley Parks was living the adventure.

The hidden room carried years of dust in the air. It filled her lungs, as if it had held its breath for decades, just waiting to exhale into the lungs of another, sharing the weight of concealment. She hesitated to step inside. It could be a trap. What if she stepped into the pocket of the house, only to be sealed up and kept secret? A warm sensation slipped over the palm of her hands. It pulled at them and lifted her arms forward. It should have been terrifying, but it was easy. There was a calm to this. Arms outstretched, she curved her hands to fit the invisible palms and let herself be led into the pocket.

They moved forward until she felt the hardness of the floor shift to a soft, paper-like crinkle. Her arms fell to her sides and the warm sensation moved away. Ripley knelt down into the dust and wiped away the residue of time from what seemed to be a large envelope.

"I can't see anything very clearly," she said.

There was silence for a moment then a rolling sound, as something came tumbling from the corner. Ripley reached out and felt for it. It was fuzzy with what she hoped was dust. She picked it up and slowly brought it close to her face to get a better look. As she realized that what she held was a wax candle, indeed very dusty, the wick flickered into a flame.

"You're prepared," she said. She felt the room, or its other occupant shrug invisible shoulders.

In the candlelight Ripley could see that it was indeed a large, yellowed envelope. She pulled away the strings that had sealed it and sitting on the floor, carefully slid the contents out onto her lap. There were three form letters with a large V, three dots, a dash, and the word MAIL printed at the bottom. At the top, there was an address for a place in New York and a return address for a local street. Ripley recognized the name, Branwyth Street. She had driven down it many times, though she couldn't recall ever having a listing there. In the middle of the papers lay the body of the letters.

The one on top read:

Dear Edgar, What is there to say? I love you. Very odd of you to ask a question and never give answer to a happy reply. I miss you. All my love. Always. Cora, October 10, 1942

The middle one read:

Dear Edgar, It has been some time and I have much to say. Though not much space to say it within these censored forms. I did not receive a response from you. I supposed my last letter would have been replied to quickly. I hope you are well, and it is just a delay in the carrier or process. Whatever the reason, my answer is the same. Yes. There are others trying to sway me from you. One in particular - who is very persistent, but my heart is yours and all the rest of me to go with it. Though, I fear I am overrated. Your mother and father are well. Sis and Caleb are looking well too. I saw them playing in the yard when I brought tomatoes to your mother. You need not worry about any of us. We will be here waiting for you. I have taken a job driving a grocery truck. It keeps me busy and allows for plenty of fresh air. Write soon.

All my love. Always. Cora, August 2, 1942

The letter underneath read:

Dear Edgar, Of course. And YES. Many times over. I do not think you overly eager by sending your request inside of Daniel's letter home, as well as yours. Good thing as I have not received your letter. I do wish you had asked in person, only so I could kiss you in reply. I would cover this paper in lipstick kisses, but I hear that is frowned upon and creates havoc with the scanning machines. Rather funny to imagine. I look forward to your return. I say we marry the very moment you get back. Perhaps on the station platform.

All my love. Always. Cora, July 5, 1942

Ripley sat in the glow of the candlelight.

"Are you Edgar?" she asked into the shadows. The warm sensation drifted over the hand holding the candle and pulled gently toward the floor. There was another envelope. A large black stain covered the bottom half of it. The warm sensation let go. Ripley picked up the envelope and ran her fingers over the ink stain. Three more letters were inside. They were smaller, scanned, not the originals. They were replies from the New York address, but Ripley guessed they were written from a lot further away than that.

The top one read:

Sweetest Cora, I do not understand why you have not replied. At least, reading 'no' from you would be better than hearing second hand that you have gone off with Oscar. His post office would do well without him. I hope he reads this and never writes to me again. Father says that it is a lie, but how can I deny a direct letter from the man himself coupled with no letter from you. I do not like it, but I wish you well. What else is there to wish for someone I still love?

Edgar, October 2, 1942.

The middle one read:

Sweetest Cora, your delay in response is too suspenseful. Please don't keep up the act. I eagerly await your reply. Mother says you brought over some tomatoes and chased Caleb and Sis around the yard. I like to imagine that. It makes me very happy to think of all of you being happy together. She also said you have taken a job driving a grocery truck. I suppose you will be delivering tomatoes to a lot of places. Don't go chasing other people's siblings. I am keeping busy here. The weather is unlike anything. I send all my best. Love till the end and onward.

Edgar, August 20, 1942

The one underneath read:

Sweetest Cora, I will keep this short. I have seen a lot of beautiful places this past year. None of them compare to you and to the thought of coming home to you. Will you do me the honor of being there for me? Will you, Cora Rylan, marry me?

All my best. Love till the end and onward.

Edgar, June 29, 1942.

"Oscar?" asked Ripley.

The candle flame flickered and nodded.

"Why would you do that?" Ripley paused.

There was silence. The flame on the candle dwindled but did not go out.

"You regret it?" she whispered.

The flame flickered and nodded.

"Did Edgar figure it out, when he came home? Did Cora set things right?"

The flame went out.

Ripley sat in the dark, suddenly aware of just how cold the house was. The fears that fled her when she reached the office were returning and filling their void.

"Oh," was her reply.

She placed the candle on the floor. She held all the letters in her hands. The warm sensation curved around her elbow and guided her to her feet.

"What should I do with them?" She shivered despite the warmth.

There was no response.

"I don't think I should deliver them. I'm not sure who I would deliver them to. Cora is probably no longer at Branwyth Street." She regretted saying that. Here was Oscar residing on Pin Row. How could she make assumptions on the whereabouts of anyone?

"Oscar, she probably thought the letters were lost. There would be no need for her to know you stopped hers from going out."

The warm sensation gave her elbow a squeeze. She felt it move down her arm to her wrist. It paused on her hand and held there for a moment. Then Ripley watched as the letters lifted from her grasp and moved off into the shadows.

"Why did you confess? Why do you trust me?" Ripley said.

"Pocket," came his voice from the corner.

She ran her fingers over her pocket.

"I need to go home."

Ripley watched the shadows for any sign of movement. None came. Then he was there. She had not felt him move out of the shadows, but he was there beside her again.

"Oscar, it was messed up. What you did—" she whispered, "but it isn't easy carrying secrets, no matter where we store them."

They moved back toward the office.

"I know people who work on houses, all sorts of people, all sorts of trades. I'm going to send someone to get rid of the ink stain. It may take a couple of days, but I'll send someone. I hope it brings you some peace."

They emerged from the pocket. She checked the frosted door pane for a sign of light. Everything remained dark.

"Pocket," he said.

Together they sealed up the hidden room. They put the books back on the shelves; secured the stamps in the encyclopedia with the mourning dove, and then he escorted her to the front doors with a warm hold on her hands. There was only a faint glow coming from the basement, as they passed the stairwell.

Before she turned to leave, Ripley timidly asked, "When I come back, will I be able to go in the basement? By myself? With you?"

"NO." His voice was loud and harsh, startling her.

"What's down there, Oscar?" Ripley motioned to go past him.

"NO," he boomed.

Quickly she turned back for the doors, reaching out for a doorknob, but the warmth seized on her hands. It pulled them back and rippled up her arms till it gripped both of her shoulders and turned from warmth to ice. She was sure that if she could see him, they would be face to face. The grip became increasingly tense. A painful pressure was building. Her frame was aching in the unseen vice. And then suddenly, he let go. There was an audible exhale, and her face was bathed in the fume of a leathery cigar. Pulse thumping rapidly in her ears, she did not wait a single second. She turned and threw open the doors, leaping out into the glow of the porch lights. The rich leather aroma leapt out the door with her.

The sound of heavy stomping moved down the hall and she thought for a moment he was retreating. Then thud upon thud pelted the walls and the stomping became a run that barreled back toward the door. Ripley shoved the doors into their frame rattling the dandelion glass. The doorknobs shook violently, as Ripley struggled to keep the doors closed and put the lockbox on. The porch lights flickered madly. The doors waged war with her. Pulling and heaving like her own lungs. Lights appeared in the windows and just as quickly went out. The windowpanes rattled until white paint slivers broke loose like tears.

When the doors were secure, Ripley Parks ran for the car, the house snarling behind her.

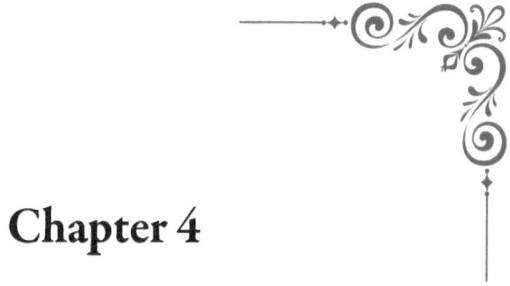

Chapter 4

November 30, 2022

"I think your account might be more terrifying than my own." Mortimer looked up at her over the magazine pages held out before him.

"I'm not sure. I mean I didn't really see anything the way you did," she replied.

"You saw enough. And perhaps you've seen things at other times."

They stared at each other for a moment, and she knew that she did not need to say anything. She may eventually, but not yet. She broke from his gaze and looked down at her purse.

"So you don't want the theater?"

"Not in the slightest," Mortimer replied.

Franley nodded, "I wouldn't either."

"What happened to the post office house?" Mortimer closed the magazine and leaned over to set it down by the hearth.

"I gave it to another realtor, who thought I was nuts to give it up. It sold to a family of four and from what I've heard, they are happy with no mention of anything at all out of the ordinary, except that the children refuse to play in their playroom."

"The playroom is in the basement?" Mortimer guessed.

"The office by the kitchen," Franley replied.

"Right," Mortimer laughed.

"Mom thought she could keep an eye on them in there while she and Dad worked in the kitchen, but well... you know." She smoothed the flap over her purse and took the last sip of her tea.

"Are you going to offer to show me your list?" Mortimer asked gently.

Franley started, jumping a little, almost rising from the chair, but caught herself and paused at the edge.

"Here, let me take that," Mortimer offered, reaching for the teacup that now hung sideways from her hand.

She handed it over with an apology. "Are you asking because I keep fidgeting with my purse, or because Alicia asked you to?"

Mortimer smiled, taking the cup and setting it by the magazine on the hearth.

"How did she know, anyway? Those methods you mentioned?" Franley wasn't sure what she was going to do next. She wanted to share the list with someone who might understand, and Mortimer might just be her chance, but at the same time sharing *her list* felt like breaking an unofficial deal with herself.

"I honestly don't know how she knew this time. Usually she just dabbles with crystals and candles, but sometimes they reach out to her."

"They?" she asked.

Mortimer nodded again. His face was gentle in the light of the fire with his mammoth eyebrows furrowed just slightly.

"Consider this, I've already seen part of it in the submission you had published in Imagine Shadows. I would have known about the list without Alicia mentioning you would have it on you. As you say, you have a tell, and you did write about it."

"Well, yes I suppose," she said feeling a little silly. "Oh, I was careful in the writing, though obviously I mentioned it."

"Yes, I have a feel for it."

"I suppose you do."

"Look, you know what happened to me and what I wrote. That's just how it went down. I changed names, sure, but other than that what you read is what you get. Truth. You changed your name too, Ripley," Mortimer replied.

"I'm a Sigourney Weaver fan," Franley said.

"Me too. So, there's another common piece of ground for us to stand on."

Franley studied him a moment longer. His soft features matched his voice. He seemed like the most trustworthy person on the planet, but if life had taught her anything, it was that those were the people you usually had to worry about. She might be sensitive to some things, but reading mortal people was not always her strong suit.

"Okay. I'll show you the list, but I need you to answer something for me first," she offered.

"Shoot. Go ahead. Anything." He relaxed in his wingback.

"Who were you glancing around for, when you let me in, before you shut the door?" Franley kept her eyes on his. He didn't flinch. He just sighed, tilted his head, and then cleared his throat. It seemed genuine like he had needed to do so; not like he was mocking her query.

"There's been someone hanging around," he replied when he had recovered his voice. "I don't know if they have any business with me. I've yet to get a very good look at them. They tend to duck just out of sight, just out of my periphery." Mortimer lifted his head and looked at the fire. He shrugged. "Ah well, that's who I was looking for, but who they are, I can't say."

Franley decided that would have to be an acceptable enough response. Without giving herself another moment to ponder the decision, she took the yellow paper from her purse and passed it to him. For what seemed like several impossibly long moments, he poured over it, appearing to read and re-read certain entries. His features fluctuated from tense to softly child-like. At one point, he even laughed.

"Are you finding me humorous?" she queried.

"No. No, my apologies. It just always amuses me when people blame racoons for house noises. I mean, really, how many times do racoons infiltrate attics and kitchen cupboards without a trace? Just picturing them running stealthily amuck tickles me. No. No, I wasn't laughing at you." He took one last look over the list. It was much longer and more detailed than what she had shared in the magazine. He passed it back to her.

"So, you don't think I'm crazy then?"

"I don't typically invite crazy people to stay for tea."

At this, Franley relaxed a little and a moment later when Mortimer's stomach began to grumble in a loud, unignorable way, she relaxed even more as he giggled in spite of himself.

"Do you feel any better, having shared the list with another Imagine Shadows alum?" he asked.

"I suppose, a little?" she replied.

"How would you like to visit the diner I mentioned in my entry? The one where I met Luella, or rather Louisa, for coffee? It's the best option, locally. I am, apparently, quite hungry."

A short walk from Mortimer's house was the best cherry pie Franley had ever had. It had been preceded by the best chicken salad sandwich she had ever had on the best croissant she had ever had. This place was legit and to top it off, the chef had turned out to be another piece of Mortimer's story. It seemed Callie, or rather Alicia, had more talents Mortimer had been waiting to reveal. She was responsible for the amazing food they had been indulging in. As the main chef, working the first shift, Alicia had come up with the recipes for each item Franley had eaten. Everything was from scratch, even the croissant. When she spied them from the back of house, she promptly delivered the food to the table herself.

"I had a feeling you might stop by," she said when she came out to deliver the sandwiches. "I'd love to talk. If that's okay? I'm just about done prepping for the next shift. I'll be out with dessert."

And so, she had come out ten minutes later with hot cherry pie.

"I don't dabble in crystals. I like the way candles smell. I collect both and though I love Mortimer as a dear old friend, he is quite stuffy when it comes to anything, well, not resolutely proper."

"Resolutely proper?" Franley shifted in her seat.

"You know, anything that might make one look like a hippie, or anything other than a well-trained member of society. I've also never been a medium in training. I'm not sure where he got that idea from." She cast a weary glance at Mortimer. "I'm sensitive and empathic and sometimes *they* do come to me, but I don't seek them out. I really didn't talk to him for a while after his story was published in Imagine Shadows. He told it well, except for the part about me being some flippant medium. Ask any of the others, they'll tell you the same. I don't know why he told it that way, except maybe he wishes he were just as intuitive and since he's not, I get to be the flighty weirdo."

She winked at Mortimer who took a sip of his coffee, raised his eyebrows, waggled them, and then averted his eyes to the window.

"Who are *they*? I have a guess, but how do you really know?" asked Franley, watching the shadows cast by the branches of a small tree outside the window, sway across the table and across her hands that were resting there. She knew if she kept them on the table, she wouldn't fidget with her purse.

"They are varied. Sometimes they are themselves, spirits of the deceased, or something clearly never human. Sometimes they are imposters. Imposters come in two varieties. There are dark beings, demons if you will. There are also what I refer to as mimics and they are more actors and jokesters. I don't know if they're like parrots, or humans, or chameleons. They are some sort of species that's really good at acting out what they see and hear. I just don't know if they are what Yoshi would refer to as scientific in nature, or more supernatural. That's to be determined, I guess."

"Yoshi, is he—"

"Hiro?"

Franley nodded.

"Yes." Alicia gave a laugh. "He is Mortimer's Hiro."

"Do you keep in touch with him too?

"You could say that. I mean, I did marry him." Alicia leaned back her in chair. "Why don't you come over? I'm heading home in a few minutes. I'll show you the crystals of controversy and you can meet Yoshi in his natural habitat."

When Franley had insisted on paying the bill, she walked with Mortimer back to his front steps, thanking him for the afternoon and for not laughing at her. She wondered silently though, if he was beginning to think of her as a flighty sort of someone, since she and Alicia evidently had a lot in common. He had said he wasn't laughing at her, but he hadn't said much more about the list either.

"I don't mean to be hard on her," he said seeming to guess her thoughts. "Alicia has always been gracious, but she does unsettle me at times. It is odd to know things that one shouldn't be capable of knowing. Sometimes I wonder if Yoshi married her as a science experiment." He attempted a smile that seemed hopeful for a reciprocated laugh.

Instead the look of her distaste at this comment compelled him to promise Franley that Alicia was like a little sister to him as he kicked at a loose piece of cement near the base of the first step. Franley began to feel a little awkward and hadn't meant to make him feel bad. He had been so gracious to spend the afternoon with her. In kind she thanked him again for the afternoon, suggested that maybe she could come again, announced her appreciation once more, and turned to go.

Mortimer stretched out a hand toward her, gently reaching for her elbow, and let it drop as she looked back over her shoulder.

"I know I'm an old man, set in his ways. And I know that she knows that we look out for each other in the end. And that's what matters, isn't it? We can agree to disagree and just love each other anyway."

Franley stopped, her autumn red hair falling across her face as she turned back toward him. "You two are lucky to know each other," she said, trusting the statement conveyed the hope he had just given her. The kindness and the truth of it were something she desperately needed.

Mortimer smiled in reply and waggled his eyebrows again, in what Franley realized must be his version of snarl face. She watched him walk back up his front steps, looking into some nearby rose bushes as he went.

Chapter 5

November 30, 2022

Not fifteen minutes later, Franley found herself in Alicia and Yoshi's front drive. *Bright. Lovingly cared for. Spacious looking.* She had taken the short drive to their home straight from Mortimer's. Alicia and Yoshi were out of the main, historic area, in a quaint neighborhood with an old, rural suburban feel with its proximity in between the university and small downtown. She had parked in their driveway and sent a short text to Bill. They were doing better because she was doing better, about letting him know that she was out and safe. He didn't mind her being gone, not that he wanted her gone, but he didn't mind it, if he knew she was safe. He didn't really understand when they discussed her list, but he had supported her writing into Imagine Shadows just as he had supported her endeavor into real estate. She reached over and tapped the top of her purse, hesitated for a moment, and then took out the list and a purple ink pen and wrote:

November 30, 2022

Mortimer Blackwood, Brownstone Residence – There are cream color roses on a bush by the front door. I saw one lift, as if plucked from the stem, and rotate before Mortimer's face. I thought he may look back at me, but he didn't. He just went inside.

The home before her now was a 1980's ranch with a large bay window that extended outward in a hexagonal frame meant to fill the main areas with light. Yoshi and Alicia had decorated the window with a drastic amount of various house plants and with what Franley presumed were Alicia's crystals interspersed throughout.

"This was Yoshi's aunt's house," Alicia said after inviting her in.

"It's beautiful. There's so much sunlight," Franley replied, looking around. Plants and crystals were everywhere. The grey afternoon had given way to a bright early evening. The crystals refracted little shafts of light across fronds and floor alike.

"She passed about six months ago." Alicia looked over her shoulder at something Franley couldn't see. Franley looked quickly away as Alicia resumed looking forward.

"She's not here." Alicia let out a small congenial laugh. "I've only seen her once since then, in a dream. We didn't really speak though, she just smiled at me and gave me Yoshi's baby blanket, a symbol for me to care for him. She was the one who raised him." She said this as if it were the most normal thing in the world to say, as if it were something that people talked about all the time, the visiting of the deceased.

Franley felt completely at ease. "That's beautiful," she replied.

"It was." Alicia walked over to the bay window.

"These crystals started because of my travels. I've loved traveling ever since I was small, and I've been collecting them just as long. They were never a new age endeavor, no matter what anyone else may think." She put an emphasis on *anyone.*

"They were pretty rocks that I collected when I traveled. I went through a brief phase where I thought maybe they were channeling something because of my increasing awareness to things, but it's not them. I did put them away for a while, but I missed them. They're just happy memories, each one. I don't pray to them. I don't ask anything of them. They just make me happy."

Franley nodded, looking around and taking it all in.

"I don't know what's on your list, Franley, just that you have one. I don't know how I know it. I don't know how I knew you would be visiting Mortimer. The thoughts just pull up and park inside my head and there's really no explanation for me to give. Sometimes I can tell good from bad and sometimes there's just a neutral tone of things being as they are and that's how I feel about your list. It just is. And if that list helps you, like my crystals help me, then I think it is a fine thing to have. You don't serve it. It serves you. You, I believe, like me, choose to serve God. And you serve Him alone."

Franley tilted her head to the side, looking up at this woman who was slightly taller than she, who knew things without explanation, who had known that Franley did indeed serve God and somehow had also known that she questioned her sensitivities in light of that. This woman did not hesitate to call it as she saw it. Though, she couldn't fathom how she had seen this side of her based on their limited interaction. She had not yet mentioned her faith, and she had not guessed Alicia's, but she was thankful for the information now and pondered if perhaps that was why she felt at ease from the moment they had met.

Alicia was looking out across the street; the sunlight casting shadows across her face from the dividing frames in the large window. Franley could see slivers of white in her otherwise dark hair that drifted over a pink sweater to her waist, stopping at the line of her floral patchwork pants.

"I don't need to know what's on that list to know you are a kindred spirit. And I don't need anyone to tell me why you're really here. You're not alone, Franley. Don't let anyone ever tell you otherwise. What you experience, whatever it may be, you are not alone. Real estate was a very clever business for you to go into–giving you access to lots of properties and people–to gauge other places and experiences." Alicia winked and smiled so warmly that Franley could not feel ashamed at her career motives being found out.

"Look around." Alicia waved at the room. "Follow me." She turned and led the way into an adjoining dining and kitchen space. "All these plants and crystals have names like you and me. Names we gave them, that people gave them, as if they were the parents naming their offspring. Silly, really. The plants and rocks had names before we ever started naming them. Maybe they were not names that we could pronounce, or hear, or understand really, but humans tend to project themselves into everything, even other forms of life. So, we give them names and thereby claim them. I feel very differently. I feel very much that I can care for something without naming it." She stroked the tendrils of a small fern by the kitchen coffee pot. "I feel that I can appreciate something without expecting anything in return." She gestured to what appeared to be rose quartz in a little terrarium next to a springy looking air plant, hanging in the window over the sink.

"What do you mean they had names, before we named them?" Franley turned slowly as she moved through the kitchen, trying to take in the overwhelming amount of greenery and glistening stones that covered all the surfaces in the most satisfying and tasteful way.

"I just mean that we didn't create them. God created them. Spoke life into them." Alicia was watching her now and smiling.

"I agree, but rocks?" Franley bent to get a closer look at an amethyst perched among some lilies.

"Well, they grow and form. They are shaped. I don't think they have life the way we do, but they do tell histories, and they can in some cases convert stress into energy. For instance, quartz in watches."

"Piezoelectric, that's the term," said a voice from behind Franley. She turned to see a tall man in a maroon t-shirt and jeans enter the room, heading for the refrigerator. His peppered hair fell slightly into his eyes. "Stress placed on a little tiny crystal tuning fork, produces the oscillation to keep time, on time. More or less. In a nutshell. Science in a crumb." He bent into the fridge and pulled out a gallon of orange juice. "Anyone else?" he proffered, subconsciously pushing his hair out of his eyes.

"Yoshi, this is Franley." Alicia gestured to her. "She's the one I mentioned was going to visit Mortimer about the theater."

"I had a hunch. It's nice to meet you, Franley. I overheard a little of your conversation, unintentionally. You should know that the fern is named Tilda. At least, that's what Alicia calls her." He winked and began to set out glasses. "Orange juice?"

For the next hour, they sat in the kitchen with orange juice and discussed the various plants and stones. Franley felt as if she had known them her whole life and Alicia and Yoshi felt the same of her. It was one of those rare moments to feel found in the midst of a lone wasteland where no one knew what to do with you and you knew not what to do with anyone else either, until suddenly you were picked up and appreciated for what you were, allowing you to reciprocate the appreciation even if it wasn't demanded to be returned.

Eventually, the conversation landed back on Mortimer and the theater. "He's not buying it, is he?" asked Yoshi.

"No, definitely not. Do you know of anyone else who would want it?" asked Franley.

"I don't know. Everyone else we worked with moved away. I don't know of anyone else around with the type of funding needed to run it. We've never been an area with heavy income, aside from the university. Alicia and I get to stay here because I work remotely, and the diner does well. Louisa's shop is profitable because it's the only general, sundries, all-purpose store around for thirty miles. It also sells amazing fudge. The diner does well and stays open because it's the only diner open for breakfast and because of Alicia's food. How far did you drive today to get here?" Yoshi replied with a swift glance at his wife to see if she was happy about his appreciation of her food. She was.

"Fifty-eight miles. At least that's what the GPS showed this morning," Franley said.

Alicia laughed. "Well, you've got a pretty good idea of what we're dealing with then. Wasn't much to see on the way, was there?"

"A lot of cows," Franley replied.

"And we like it that way," said Yoshi. "Still, it would be a shame to see the theater fall into disrepair."

For the first time since they had sat down the conversation faded away into silence. Faintly, Franley could hear a clock ticking and wondered if there might be a tiny bit of quartz pushing the sound into existence. Alicia stared out the window and Yoshi fidgeted with his nearly empty juice, tilting the tiny, remaining drops into a slow rotation around the bottom ring of the glass. Eventually, with a sniffle and sigh, he sat up straighter, adjusting his weight in the chair.

Alicia glanced at him, reading his intentions. She gave him a nudge. "Franley has read the story that Mortimer wrote. In fact, she has one of her own in the magazine too."

Yoshi took the opportunity that had been cleared for him. "Did Mortimer tell you that I have an entry in Imagine Shadows?" He looked at Franley with a mix of distaste and humor, though she could tell the expression was not directed at her.

"No, he didn't," she replied, also adjusting her weight in the chair and sitting up straighter. "I had no idea. What date are you?" She glanced at Alicia, who was now looking down into her glass and did not seem like she wanted to look elsewhere.

"July 11, 2013."

"Two years before Mortimers," Alicia murmured without looking up.

"That's when it got published, anyway. I sent in the story months beforehand, much like how Mortimer's story took place in 2001, but he didn't submit and have it published until 2015. The happening, I submitted, was long ago, when I was young. There wasn't really anyone to talk to about it. As an adult, I found the magazine in a waiting room at a dermatologist's office. Fortunately, I had a long wait and had time to read it almost cover to cover. Enough time for me to find out that there were others like me, others who needed some place to tell their stories and to be taken seriously, or at least not be scoffed at. By the time I was participating at the theater, I also had a full career analyzing plankton."

"Analyzing plankton?" Franley interrupted. "That's not something I would have guessed." She leaned forward enthusiastically. "Can you do that remotely, now?"

"Sort of. I'm in IT now, but every now and then I get sent something to look over from the university," Yoshi replied.

"A man of many trades," Alicia added, at last looking up.

"Anyways, I wrote into the magazine because I didn't know if I could say anything to my family. I didn't want my colleagues, mostly a bunch of skeptical, hands of science above all else types, to respect me less. I couldn't say anything to them. Perhaps, it's the same reason I gravitated toward IT after what went down in Mortimer's story. I had a feeling that I was going to need more space to be myself if I desired. So, I took a step away from hard science," Yoshi said.

"Are there not a lot of skeptics in IT," asked Franley.

"There are all types in that field," said Yoshi. "It's a good fit for most anyone, as far as believing and skepticizing, or being nerdy or posh, or whatever you want to be really. It's logical, sure, but you're allowed to imagine inside of it. Imagining inside of hard science can get you *in trouble* or stall your career advancement. Actually, I probably should have gone into quantum mechanics, there's more room there to—I am now rambling," Yoshi paused. "My apologies," he said, beginning to look more serious. "I get carried away."

"No need to apologize," Franley said. "I understand. I really do." She tapped her purse that was hanging on the back of her chair. "It took me a long time to tell anyone. Ages. And I'm married to a school counselor," she laughed. "Do you have a copy of your story? I'd love to know it. Maybe, I've already read it. Probably, I have."

"We have a copy, but if it's alright, I could just tell it to you?" Yoshi replied.

"Even better," Franley said.

Yoshi bent his head into his palm, his fingers climbing up through his hair. He gave a small shake of his head and then pulled his hand away, his fingers letting his hair fall in a disheveled fringe across his eyes.

Chapter 6

Alicia and Yoshi's Kitchen Table
   November 30, 2022
   Recycled Time
   by Yoshi V.

"It was the kind of day that made it hard to think about anything other than the day itself; clear, bright, warm, with the feeling that nothing existed, but nature and everything to be seen within it. I was fifteen. I had spent the day outside in my grandparents' yard, which was quite large at about ten acres. It was partly wooded, so I had spent some time wandering trails and had even attempted to make my own at one point. Late in the afternoon, I fell asleep after crawling under a picnic table, close to the stone patio at the back of their house. I hadn't really intended to sleep at all, but I must have been exhausted because I was out for close to two hours. I don't remember dreaming. The grass was cool under the table and there were ants lined up under one of the boards of the tabletop. I lay there looking at them and then drifted off.

When I woke, I was laying on my left side with my arms pulled up and my fists touching together against my chest. I rolled onto my back and saw the underside of the tabletop was free of ants. I could hear crickets and was aware of the hour being later because my surroundings were dim. I turned my head to the right, saw the patio, the pants and shoes of my grandfather at his grill, caught the smell of charcoal and hot dogs, and rolled the rest of the way over onto my right side. I smiled at the thought of hot dogs and then I opened my eyes. I was laying on my left side with my arms pulled up and my fists touching together against my chest. I rolled onto my back and saw the underside of the tabletop was free of ants. I could hear crickets and was aware of the hour being later because my surroundings were dim. I turned my head to the right, saw the patio, the pants and shoes of my grandfather at his grill, caught the smell of charcoal and hot dogs, and rolled the rest of the way over onto my right side. I smiled at the thought of hotdogs and then I opened my eyes. I was laying on my left side with my arms pulled up and my fists touching together against my chest. I rolled onto my back and saw the underside of the tabletop was free of ants. I could hear crickets and was aware of the hour being later because my surroundings were dim. I turned my head to the right, saw the patio, the pants and shoes of my grandfather at his grill, caught the smell of charcoal and hot dogs, and rolled the rest of the way over onto my right side. I smiled at the thought of hot dogs and waited, wondering if I was about to recycle again.

I do not know what happened, except that I lived the exact same moment three times consecutively. The movements, the sights, the smells, the emotion—all of it—three times in a row. Time replayed itself, reset itself, or I got off at this stop in the multiverse. To this day, I have not come across another encounter like it. I'd love to talk to someone who has also had an experience like this, but I haven't found them.

Telling anyone seemed to be out of the question. I was a silly fifteen-year-old boy, who fell asleep under a picnic table, and crawled out from under it, dirty and sweaty and asking about hot dogs. So, I kept it to myself. For years, I did research on the side and in some ways the event led me to studying plankton, but I don't need to get into all that. Suffice it to say, my scrutiny started with ants and went toward even smaller creatures. And no, I don't think tiny creatures are responsible for my experience, but then again who knows. *If* ants, *Then* time glitch? It doesn't look that way.

THE CONSEQUENT

I've heard of stories, some in Imagine Shadows even, where people walk into a different time. For example, people who witness battles on battlefields that haven't seen war for a century. There are those who talk about visiting a building where the people inside of it interact with them, but are dressed in an outdated way and maybe even talk in an outdated way, but sometimes these are historical places, so the visitors think it is a re-enactment, only to find out later there was no such re-enactment and in some cases the entire building hasn't existed for years, but it did in fact exist at one point in history and the way it existed does in fact mesh with what they experienced.

These time slips, or overlaps, are different though. What I lived was my time, my moment, just replaying in three consecutive motions. It was like being reset, but without knowing that I was being reset. I didn't put myself back onto my left side with my fists touching, after I had rolled onto my right. I had no desire to even do that. I was a hungry fifteen-year-old whose grandfather was feet away with his favorite food. Yet, it happened. I reset and time replayed."

"I wish I had something similar to share with you," Franley replied when Yoshi seemed to have finished his story. "It's incredibly fascinating. The closest I can come to that, is admittedly not close at all. It's like the other stories, the time slips, maybe. When I was in kindergarten, my family used to drive past a brown barn with white doors. It was on the way to school and on the way to church. I saw it almost every day of the week. It wasn't until I was in third grade that it disappeared. One day, on the way to school, it was just gone. It had been there the day before, but then nothing. No lumber debris, no dead grass where it had been. There was just the same green field where I always saw it, only no barn. I asked my parents about it, but they had no idea what I was talking about. I asked other kids at school. No one knew of the barn. I got accused of making it up and was more or less asked to shush it. No more barn talk, which I guess was only fair because I had harped on it for a month by then."

"A ghost barn," Yoshi replied. "But yes, not the same. Still, funny isn't it—that you could see it for years and then one day not? It's difficult to make sense of so much of what we experience as individuals and collectively."

"Have you ever experienced anything like either?" Franley asked, looking to Alicia.

"I haven't, actually," she replied. "I guess I've been limited to full body apparitions, voices, dreams, and being given information I didn't seek out."

"Not exactly limiting," Yoshi said.

"True, not exactly limiting, or limited. Just different." Alicia pushed away from the table and stretched her arms upward then back down, stifling a yawn. "I guess we're all just little mystery boxes of different abilities."

"You were probably up really early for work. My apologies for staying late," Franley said, realizing just how dark the sky outside had become. At least she had messaged Bill before coming inside this time.

"Oh no, you don't need to go. I have the day off tomorrow. I love the diner, but I will take a day of rest," said Alicia stifling another yawn, which lead to a string of sympathetically induced yawn stifling around the table.

"Well, I should be heading out soon anyway. How long have you worked at the diner?" Franley asked.

"Thirteen years. It's my day job, as Mortimer would say," Alicia replied.

Franley rose from her chair and nodded remembering the scene wherein Alicia dubbed Callie had stormed off to the theater bathrooms declaring her lack of a day job when Lousia dubbed Luella had sold the theater.

Eager not to start in on Mortimer, she changed the subject. "Circling back a second, it is funny you mention mystery boxes." Franley pushed in her chair. "My kids love those. I bought a couple of them this morning. They're mystery animal plush with magnets in their feet. They're both going to be hoping for the polar bear. I tried looking up the SKU numbers. Sometimes people have made charts to help you cheat at figuring out what's in the box. I know it kind of defeats the purpose."

A phone began to buzz from somewhere in the house. Without saying a word, Alicia stood and left the kitchen, heading off toward the back of the house.

"Did you find the SKU for the bear?" Yoshi asked, also rising from his chair.

"No, there wasn't a chart for this one." Franley slipped her purse onto her shoulder and patted down the flap. "It's been really nice this evening. I appreciate you both letting me hang out and talk for a while and I am sorry if I have overstayed."

"Not at all," Yoshi replied. We eat late. You can stay for dinner, if you like.

"I should be getting back, but thank you and—"

Alicia came running back into the room with her cell phone clutched tightly in her fist.

"Can you get into the theater?" said Alicia.

"I have a key. Why?" Franley said, taking in the panic Alicia was putting out.

"That was Louisa. She was on her way home, driving past, and said that all the lights are on. She tried calling Mortimer, but he didn't answer. She tried you, Yoshi, but I guess your phone is on silent," said Alicia.

Yoshi took his phone out of his pocket and held it up to show there was indeed a missed call.

"Well, it's probably someone from the university. They still have a key until it is sold," Franley offered, unsure of what the fuss was about.

"I would agree with you, but Dugan is the one who keeps it and he's out of the country for the next two days." Alicia looked at Franley with confusion. "Right?"

"You're right, absolutely right," Franley said a little caught off guard at her forgetfulness and at Alicia's knowledge. "He is away. Yes."

"She's in a book club with some of his colleagues. That's how she knows about his going ons," Yoshi said, guessing at Franley's expression. "I'll go over and check it out," he offered. "But I will need you to let me in."

"I don't like that." Alicia stepped forward and grabbed his arm, putting herself between him and Franley. She looked in his face, pleading for some other option.

"I'll call the non-emergency number and have someone check it out. I'll wait for them in my car. No one else needs to go," Franley said, watching.

"Well, I don't like the idea of you sitting out there by yourself either," said Alicia, turning to her, still holding onto Yoshi.

"It's really not the best idea, Franley," he added. "Cars regularly get broken into downtown. It's not too serious, except I don't know if anyone would try anything—well, if they would try to steal from your vehicle with you seated in it—especially by yourself."

It was the same old thing, like a disembodied voice that hovers behind the ear, calling out even when you've moved forward and haven't wanted to remember it exists, this necessity of not being a woman alone, a woman in the dark.

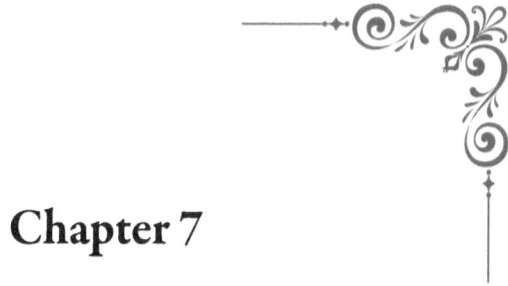

Chapter 7

November 30, 2022

Such was the position of a woman's solitude that out of fear three people could find themselves preserving their company and if they were honest, their curiosity, in Franley's car. Bill and the kids joined them by speakerphone for a short bit, after they had called the non-emergency number on the way. Alicia had messaged Louisa, who called Mortimer, to say that they were having it checked out. Franley had messaged Dugan before calling the non-emergency number to see if perhaps he had given the key to someone else. He had not responded. She wasn't sure what time zone he was in and thought perhaps he may be asleep. She didn't feel guilty about potentially waking him though. He had sent her a few uncanny text messages at various hours after she had taken the listing.

"So, what is the deal with Mortimer and Louisa? Are you close with them, besides the theater connection? If that is completely none of my business, please forget I asked," Franley faltered. She wasn't used to blurting out questions of that nature, the nature of which could be construed as gossip, but the meet-up at the diner had caused her to wonder what the nature of their friendship really was.

Alicia, all too happy to keep talking while the lit theater cast its shadow over the car, answered easily. "We are close. We were friends because of our acting together. It is where we all met. Well, actually, Louisa knew Mortimer from their childhood school days, but they got closer once she bought the theater building and he started participating

79

in the plays. It's such a small town, it would have been hard for us not to remain close, besides some shared events are bound to form unbreakable bonds."

"The Imagine Shadows story *was* obnoxious in that it exaggerates our personas, as I'm sure you've picked up on," Yoshi added, "but it was me that had put off admitting anything to anyone. I was still functioning under the idea that I could be crazy, or at minimum mentally unsettled. The haunting parts of the story are true, every bit, but I never held Alicia as if I were holding an alligator. I was fond of her immediately when we first met and I was rather grateful that she clung to me when, quite literally, everything went sideways."

"Yoshi may not have seen what went down that last night when just Mortimer and I were locked in, but he saw *me,* and I saw that he *saw* me when I came running out of those doors." Alicia gestured to the double doored front entrance. "It is true. All of it."

"You don't have to convince me," Franley said, "I already believed you."

"Oh, we know," Yoshi replied. "It's just nice to say it. Sometimes it helps me to affirm it verbally."

The lights of the surrounding buildings and streetlamps were lit at varying degrees. The streetlamps held older incandescent bulbs, which if asked, anyone in Franley's car would have said were much more pleasant than new LEDs. Some of the buildings, snuggled close by, were glowing warmly, like a 24-hour medical clinic a block away. Others were lit only by *Closed* signs, or small interior lights for security. There was a bar nearby with dim, but warmly hung outdoor lights strung over a closed patio. Two blocks away in the opposite direction of the clinic stood a rather large building, rectangular, but also rounded at the top. Its many windows were lit sporadically.

"What is that tall building, over there?" asked Franley.

"That is the Inventes, a hotel," said Yoshi. "It's as old as our theater here. The bricks around each of their doorways are even from the same batch. It seems to do well by holding conventions. It's been updated a couple times in the last few decades. The last remodel was spring, two years ago. I think."

"You seem very well up to date on all the places around," Franley said. "I'm in real estate and I didn't even know what it was."

"You're not from here though, so that makes sense," said Yoshi.

"I only live an hour away and I got the call to sell the theater," Franley replied. "I could stand to do a little more homework."

"Well, the theater was its own piece of work. I think we can forgive you for not expanding much past it," Alicia offered. "Besides, the Inventes orders food from the diner to serve in the snack stations they have on each floor. I even prepped a new batch of muffins for them to pick up before I left work this evening."

She was sitting in the back seat. Yoshi was sitting in the front passenger seat so that anyone approaching could see a man in the car, so they would know that Franley was not alone.

A thought suddenly occurred to Franley. "Have either of you been back inside the theater, since that last night, the night it was agreed to be sold?"

There was a pause for a moment. Yoshi inhaled heavily, but Alicia spoke first.

"None of us, to my knowledge, have been back." She leaned her head against the car window, eyeing the front doors. Yoshi was watching her, exhaling.

"We discussed it a few times, collectively. We would circle the idea when the school would have plays, but in the end, we always decided against it. After a few years went by, we hardly ever brought it up."

"And now, I'm kicking up the dust," Franley said, feeling a little dejected.

"The dust was kicked a long time ago. We may not have been back, but Dugan was a regular. He really did play the piano phenomenally by all accounts, but just that one. Just *that* piano. Lousia has a piano and when he came over one day close to Christmas, when we were all there, he tried to play it at Mortimer's request. It didn't go well. He fumbled terribly," said Yoshi.

"Would he have faked being bad at it? I get the impression that he and Mortimer are very much at odds," said Franley.

"Oh, they are, but it turns out that he's a distant cousin of Louisa's, so she and Dugan have tried to connect and get to know each other and learn more about their extended family. It's usually rough, but Lousia really does try, and I think Dugan does too. They're just sitting on very different branches of the tree," Alicia added.

"Is there anything special about the theater's piano? I mean, does it seem different somehow?" Franley asked.

"It's an old, four pedaled, upright, oak piece with beautiful tiger stripe wood grain, and some scroll work with doves and ribbons. The four pedals make it a little special in that it can sound like other instruments when those are used. It can sound sort of harpsichord like, but it's not a one of a kind. I don't guess. Although, the keys are different now. Dugan put some odd silver quartz overlay on them. He showed us some pictures when he was at Louisa's. He said he used the same quartz in some of the details at the Inventes when he was consulted for the remodel."

"Sorry, but did you see that?" Franley's attention had diverted, and she missed the last of what Yoshi had said.

She had been eyeing the ticket booth to the right of the doors while he spoke. The window was curtainless and the booth itself was without light, but for a moment there had been a flicker of blue, a short buzz of cyan, around the microphone that existed for the booth employee to speak into. The door from the booth into what Franley knew to be the lobby was now backlit around the edges, but she could not remember if it had been that way upon their arrival.

"See what?" asked Yoshi.

"I saw it," Alicia murmured. She started to say more, hesitated with a catch in her breath, then asked, "Franley, have you been in the theater?"

Franley did not want to answer this question. Normally, she was thorough. Normally, she knew every crevice of a place she was selling. She deemed it her responsibility to her clients to know and share the knowledge of perks and defects alike. "Well, I have been in the lobby." She looked at Alicia in the rearview mirror. "That's as far as I got."

"Did you see it, or did you feel it?" Alicia asked.

"Both," Franley replied. "Both. There was a darkness at the doors to the house, and I don't know exactly how I was seeing it, but yes, it was there. I felt it too, unlike anything else. I didn't think I could proceed. Dugan was the one with me, to show me around. He went to the doors, even as I reached out for him to try to say something, to stop him because I felt responsible, even though I didn't know why— I didn't know why I should. I guess because I could see something that he couldn't, or if he could he didn't seem bothered by it. He kept insisting I would be impressed with the lighting, but when he opened a door on the left—I swear something breathed. I think it was the house." Franley stopped, realizing just how much she had said.

Alicia put her hand on Franley's shoulder. "I get it. Yoshi does too. We believe you."

"Tell me what you saw just now," Franley asked her. Yoshi turned to look at his wife.

"I saw a blue light around the microphone—a glow like something you would see from a distant television set, but not something you would usually see straight on, except you and I both saw it straight on, just now."

"What was it?" Franley whispered.

"I wish I knew." Alicia squeezed Franley's shoulder, withdrew her hand, and touched Yoshi's face. "I think you know," she said looking into his eyes with a conviction he could not look away from.

"Why do you say that?" he asked, putting his hand on hers, "Why would I know?"

"Because you saw it at my back, when I ran out of the doors just as I saw it reflected in the window of a car that was parked in front of you. When you grabbed hold of me, I could feel you looking for it. You *saw* me, but you also *saw*, if only for a moment, what I see, the way that I see it and you knew, just as you know now that there's more to all of this."

Franley, who had been looking intently at them both, turned her eyes away. She felt she was imposing on a deeply personal moment and had not been ready for the emotion found there. She wasn't great with emotions. She was the wife who stayed out late without thinking of calling. *Getting better though!* She was the mother who never baked a cake and told her young children goodnight from the couch. She had been checking on them after they were asleep. *Getting better!*

"I've always known there was more. I just don't normally see it, but that doesn't mean I don't believe it. It also doesn't mean that I know what it is, though I did see them with you before." Yoshi's voice seemed far away to Franley now.

"That's not what I mean. I know you believe because you have seen and for other reasons, but I like that you saw beyond them even when I didn't, and I would want you to tell me when you do see whatever they are—" Alicia was replying in a scramble that made no sense to Franley, but her voice was so faint.

"I see. You see. We all see the beams." It was as if the volume had been cranked back up and had gone past the normal setting and tone. In Franley's ears, Alicia suddenly sounded almost angry.

"What beams?" Franley asked, turning back to them. They both turned their eyes to her and dropped their hands from each other. Neither seemed to understand what she was saying.

"What beams?" she asked again in case they had not heard her clearly.

"I don't know what you mean," Alicia replied with concern.

"You just said, 'We all see the beams.' What beams?" Franley's voice trailed off at her query, seeing that Alicia's face was so full of concern now that something clearly was not right. Yoshi didn't look much better. "You didn't say that. Did you?" Franley asked. She gave a deep sigh as Alicia shook her head. They all turned their attention back to the exterior of the theater.

The building was on a corner with angled architecture lines, so that the entrance and ticket booth sat further forward than the sides that sloped away. It was predominantly brick, with some cement work halfway up featuring scrolling ribbons that slightly resembled fish caught in tight little waves. The top section beyond the cement work featured more brick and an oval stained-glass window. The glass was held in an iron frame and floated within itself as a creamy, undulating lavender with an iron bar going horizontally across the middle. Franley had decided upon first inspection that it was not a very attractive window, but looking at it in the dark, backlit from within, it took on a certain quality that, while not appealing, was not repulsive either.

There were other windows, rectangular, trailing off down the right side of the building at various heights that could be seen from where they sat. These were not particularly of any notice except that the brickwork was different and Franley was not sure what part of the interior they might belong to. She had been told the theater was one story and while the odd oval window looked down into the lobby, she was not sure where the other windows might look into, except maybe offices, or storage rooms.

"There isn't an upstairs to the theater, right?" she asked.

"No, there's just the lobby and house with their high ceilings. Our theater is small by comparison to just about any other. Those second floor and up windows down the side," he gestured to the rectangular ones, guessing what Franley was getting at, "those are apartments."

"Apartments?" Franley gasped.

"Yes, wouldn't you like to rent one?" Yoshi laughed.

"You could share one with a university student," Alicia added with a smile. "That's who normally rents them."

"I had no idea. Do they have any *issues*?" Franley asked, feeling weird saying it out loud even though her present company had made it more than clear that saying these things aloud was completely acceptable.

"Doubt it." The louder voice bopped off right in her ear this time.

Seeing the look on Franley's face, though she was trying hard to keep a straight one, Alica leaned over and murmured, "What did it say?"

"Doubt it," Franley replied, looking into Alicia's eyes for an answer that didn't seem to be there.

Before anyone could say more, headlights swept over the car and across the parking lot, coming to a rest on the ticket booth window. The officer in the police cruiser waved to them, flipped off his headlights, and turned off the car. He was at Yoshi's window in a matter of moments.

"Franley Parker?" he said knocking on the window. His voice was even and gentle, and a little tired. Yoshi rolled down the window and motioned to Franley in the driver seat.

"Good evening." The officer nodded. "You called in that no one should be here? Did you check the lock box to see if the key is inside?" His mouth twitched and he sniffled.

"Well, we–no. There isn't a lockbox for this type of listing," sighed Franley. "The man who has the extra key is out of town. I'm the only other person with a key and that key is in my bag."

The officer glanced over the front of the building and side eyed the alleyway. "Alright, my name is Maxwell, and I'm going to walk around and check the doors. If they are locked, I'll need to borrow the key to go in and check it out with your permission."

"Of course," Franley replied, glancing at the department patch on his shirt. The officer walked off to check the doors and Franley reached for her purse she had wedged between her seat and the driver side door. Yoshi and Alicia watched as Maxwell pulled at the front doors, which did not budge. He checked the frame and the locks, looked over the ticket booth window, then procuring a flashlight from his belt, headed down the side into the alleyway.

Alicia turned her attention back to Franley, becoming aware that she was still rummaging through her bag. "Is the key missing?" she asked.

"No. No, I found the key. It's just that, my list—my list is—," Franley's voice was raspy and small. "It's not. Oh. Oh wait. Never mind." she said. "I thought it was gone," she whispered.

Alicia said nothing. Franley wanted her to say something. She wasn't sure what, but something surmounting understanding of the panic she had just felt. This silence unsettled her. It seemed a confirmation that they were about to face a summit of sorts, but of what she could not be sure.

Maxwell came back up the alley toward them, shaking his head.

"Should there be more than one officer? Just in case someone did break in?" said Franley to Yoshi, trying to think of normal, reasonable precautions for the type of intruders she knew were not actually inside. This, she felt, would be like Pin Row. There would be something there when she went back in and it would be something she did not like and if it were human, it would not be mortal.

"Small town department, late in the day— he's probably the only one on the clock," Yoshi replied in a low voice. "Sorry, I know that's not what you wanted to hear," he added.

"Even in a semi-college town?" asked Franley.

"Budget issues like everyone else," whispered Yoshi. "The university has its own security."

Reaching Yoshi's window, Maxwell leaned over it and glanced around at the three agitated people in the car. His brow furrowed and his mouth twitched. He sniffled.

"Okay, well I suppose I'm going in," he said, his face reflecting a deep resignation.

They were all looking back at him now and wondering if they too were about to resign themselves to the same *suppose I'm going* part of his statement.

"May I borrow that key?" he asked.

"Of course, here it is," said Franley, reaching in front of Yoshi to hand it over. Maxwell leaned down and took the key with a nod and a forced smile. He stood up straight and turned to face the theater, as the others turned in their seats to face it with him. The lights had gone out. Only the exterior light of the streetlamps remained. All the windows were dark. The ticket booth was not backlit. The oval window did not glow from within. Even the apartment windows were without their lights. The lights of the surrounding buildings remained on. The patio lights at the bar down the street were swinging in the breeze like dimly calling beacons of normalcy.

No one said a word. If asked, they could not have relayed if they had even breathed during the space that hung between the moment the lights had gone out and the moment the first of the apartment lights reappeared. Slowly, one by one, the apartments flickered back into the night from behind the shades and curtains veiling their residents. The theater remained dark. Maxwell cleared his throat, mumbled something about the grid and adjusted his belt. Feigning a casual swagger, he made his way to the double-doored entrance.

They watched Maxwell put the key in the left-hand door and make his way inside, propping the door open with some playbills he found on a chair just inside the door. They waited for a light to flick on, but none came. In silence they waited for something to happen. Ten minutes went by, and nothing did. There was no sound from within the theater that they could discern, no light, no sign of Maxwell. Another ten minutes went by with nothing to speak of. At this juncture Alicia took her phone out of her pocket and sent a text to Louisa.

Going inside. Called non-emergency number. Deputy Maxwell went in and hasn't come out. I'd like to go in by myself, but I doubt that's going to happen. Things are already at play. Watch the ledge. She added an emoji to lighten the vibe, the one with the monocle.

She was right, there was no way that Yoshi, or even Franley were going to let her enter on her own. Yoshi rolled up his window and they exited the car. Franley reached into her purse and finding her key fob, pushed the button to lock the car doors. A low beep resounded and whooped into the darkness.

They stopped in the open doorway, the scent of the old space wafting around them—something akin to pine, moth balls, and caramel laced chlorine.

"Macbeth? Really?" Franley winced looking down at the playbills wedged under the door.

"What for? Right?" Alicia smirked. "Some people never learn."

With a collective inhale and exhale they stepped across the threshold and into the theater.

It was hard to see anything for a moment. The only window into the lobby was the odd oval above, but it didn't provide any light from the darkened sky outside. The only current source of light came from the open door behind them and the streetlamps beyond. Yoshi caught his foot on the chair that the playbills had been on. He didn't fall, but the chair scraped sideways and made a small sound across the wall as it moved. Franley jumped a little, but she did not think that anyone noticed. She could barely see them ahead of her. Using the chair as a prop to steady himself toward the wall, Yoshi felt for the light switch, found it, flipped it, and the overhead chandelier burst into a low glow, revealing cream color walls crested with faint shadows from the chandelier chain. Large metal, golden palm fronds were fixed on the wall between the two sets of windowless house doors. There was a small pink, velvet sofa below them with curved arms. The carpet beneath their feet was red and just as Mortimer had described in his story, there was a small fountain in the center of the room with tiny purple tiles and two stone swans.

"Just the same," Yoshi said. He joined the women, now standing near the fountain. He put his arm around Alicia.

"Just the same," she replied.

"Did they ever fix the fountain?" Franley asked, walking toward the sofa and turning back to take the room in from that side, remembering that Mortimer in his story had said the fountain did not work.

"I'm not sure," Yoshi said. "I hope so. It would be nice."

The sentiment caught Franley a little off guard. It was nice to know she wasn't the only one who longed for historic preservation even in unsettling sorts of places.

"It's wet," said Alicia who was no longer looking at it, but staring off toward the house doors on the left. She walked over to them, as Yoshi and Franley both looked down at the fountain. It did indeed have small drops of water and smears that looked like the remnants of a splash. Yoshi reached out to touch the edge of the pool, but stopped, second guessing the idea. He withdrew his hand suddenly feeling as though it may not be water after all, though what it would be instead he could not and did not want to conceive.

"We should find Maxwell," Alicia murmured. The other two nodded. "These doors aren't budging, but I don't think he's in there. Franley, will you check the other pair of house doors?"

Franley agreed and found that they were closed tight and unwilling to budge.

"We stay together," Yoshi said. "Since, we can't get in there. We'll start on the left."

"What's on the left," asked Franley.

"Should just be restrooms and a hall for hanging coats and umbrellas," said Yoshi.

There was a door to the left and another on the right side of the lobby. Those two doors, plus the double entrance from outside, two sets of double house doors, and the one to the ticket booth made for nine doors and six possible ways to enter the room. Franley noted each door, one by one, as she moved to join Yoshi and Alicia at the left side. They pushed that door open, which swung easily and were relieved to find a stopper inside the hall. Yoshi placed it under the foot of the door. The low glow from the lobby seeped into the hall lined with coat racks and ornate wall lamps in a row on each side, all of which were off. Alicia reached up to the first lamp and pressed a button on the plate. It beamed on, illuminating a crystal sconce patterned with small roses and ivy. Yoshi moved to the opposite side of the hall and did the same. One by one they walked down the hall, pressing each lamp into life. Franley watched until they had reached the end, which only took a moment because it was not a long space. She walked between the illuminated walls and empty coat racks feeling very much that things could not get more unsettling than they were right now, with the red carpet underfoot turning burgundy in the dim lights, with the rose and ivy casting odd shapes across the walls and across their faces, knowing that this place had a history, and feeling it in her bones and in the air, which seemed inevitably to vibrate higher and hum louder with each lamp she passed.

"Maxwell?" Alicia pushed on the door to the women's restroom. The light inside flickered on. Yoshi caught the look on Franley's face as she approached.

"It does that," he said. "It's a motion sensor. At least, it used to be."

Franley smiled in spite of herself and smoothed her hand across her purse resting against her side. "Of course," she laughed slightly.

Yoshi pushed on the door to the men's room, "Maxwell?" The light flickered on in the men's room.

There was no answer from either side. They entered the women's room first, starkly white and bright in comparison to the hallway. There were three stalls, all of which were empty. Three sinks stood directly opposite the stalls with old-fashioned knobs like four-petaled flowers, two apiece for hot and cold water. They made their way through quickly and left for the men's room.

"Maxwell?" Yoshi called again, pushing the door open. As before, no answer came. It was supplied the same as the women's side except for a urinal on the far wall and a small window up at the very top that could be propped out toward the side street.

"Odd to have a window in here and not in the women's room, isn't it?" asked Franley.

"This whole place is odd," said Yoshi. "It's not exactly up to modern safety codes."

Exiting the men's room they found themselves in the dark. Every light in the hall had been turned off except for one. It beckoned, mildly flickering, at the end of the hall to the right of the door. The door was now closed. The rose and ivy patterned sconce, backlit by the bulb, cast shadows that stretched and warped across the wall in an undulating flicker.

Wasting no time, Alicia went to the lamp closest to her on the left and pressed the button. Quickly, she went down that side and lit each one, then motioned for the others to join her at the door. The stopper that had been holding the door open to the lobby when they entered the restrooms was nowhere to be seen.

They waited a moment, listening and hearing nothing. Yoshi put his hands on the door and pushed slowly. As he did so there was a tiny plink of sound behind them. Turning in unison, they found the first lamp that Alicia had turned on by the men's room had gone out. A succession of tiny plinks rolled toward them as each lamp went out one by one in nearly the same rhythm and urgent pacing in which she had turned them on. The rose and ivy shadows stretched more with each lamp that went out, distorting the walls and the floor and their faces.

Not waiting for the last one to darken, Yoshi pushed the door open and rushed Alicia and Franley forward, followed them, and let the door swing behind. The stopper lay in the lobby near the fountain. Alicia ran to it, kicked it over to Yoshi, who stuffed it quickly with his feet under the door. They were all thinking it probably wouldn't make a difference but sometimes gestures and action alleviate the mind and so they paused to catch their breath, silently debating their next move.

Franley was beginning to wonder why any of them were there. She knew she was partially responsible for this listing, at least in the eyes of her clients. However, she wasn't required to be here inside of it at this moment. They had called the police. She wasn't required to respond by going inside too. As for the others, she wasn't sure why they were there at all. Yes, they had wanted to accompany her for her safety, but they also didn't have to come inside. All three of them could have remained in the parking lot. They could have called the emergency number and asked for someone else to check on Maxwell. In the pit of her gut and in some deeper fiber that doesn't have a name, it registered there was no other option because most likely no one else would understand and even if they did understand they may not be willing to admit it. So, here they were, chasing down the very person they had called for help when she was sure they all knew that they never should have called anyone. If they had just let things be, most likely nothing would have happened. She could have gone home and would most likely be brushing her teeth or pulling back the covers to climb into bed. There would be no need for concern. She could choose not to work with Dugan and the university on the sale. She wouldn't have to feel guilty about any of it. Maxwell would probably be relaxing at the station, or out patrolling, or whatever things he would normally do on a quiet small-town night. Yoshi and Alicia would be finishing up their late dinner. They were probably very hungry by now and she felt guilty about that too and wondered if she had any crackers in her purse.

As her mind traveled through the mess they had made, the rose and ivy shadow stretched from under the door, its pattern twisting and extending. She watched it reach out a full two feet from the door before coiling back and rolling up like a tendril, pulling its leaves and buds into itself and disappearing back into the hall.

"I've never been any place like this," she said. "I'm so sorry."

"What for?" said Alicia. "We knew what we were getting into, coming here. I knew from the moment we pulled up that this was not going to be easy."

"What exactly wasn't going to be easy?" asked Franley, who picked up a lilt in the end of Alicia's voice.

"Coming back," she replied. "I just meant that whatever was going to happen when we came back, wasn't going to be easy." She exchanged a look with Yoshi.

"I shouldn't have let you come back. Let's get Maxwell and go, if he's even still here." Franley wasn't sure why she added that last part. She looked hard at her new friends.

"Why would he be somewhere else?" she asked half laughing, half questioning her own statement.

Neither of them looked directly at her.

"Why would he be somewhere else?" she repeated.

"We didn't say—" began Yoshi.

"I know. I'm the one who said it, but why? Why would I think he might be somewhere else?" Franley was feeling indignant. This was too much. She didn't know why she said it, or where the thought had come from as it manifested itself upon leaving her lips and yet she knew it to be a true possibility, somehow.

Alicia seated herself on the pink sofa and gripped its edges. "Sometimes people go missing. Sometimes they start here and end up somewhere else. I know Maxwell is still here."

Franley was only partly taken aback by this information. At this point in her life she presumed it was normal not to be taken aback by such things. "You sense that he is still here?"

"I know because Louisa hasn't called me," Alicia answered staring at Franley with an expression of one bracing for impact.

"Why would Louisa call you?"

"Because she is watching the location that sometimes finds whomever the theater loses."

There was a long pause in which no one said anything. Franley watched the door to the hall and saw the stopper begin to wiggle just slightly, either that or her eyes were not pairing well with the lighting in the room.

"Should we have started with that location?" Franley at last replied, feeling completely irate at the idiocy of the situation.

"The doors were not co-operating," Yoshi interjected.

"Why not? Is the location in the house? It sounded like it was somewhere out of the theater." Franley was considering marching wherever it was the moment she found out. Maybe it would get her home faster.

"Remember the building you asked about, the Inventes?" he replied.

"Yes."

"It's a window on the fourth floor. Sometimes something ends up on the outside ledge."

"The outside ledge?"

"Yes, and before you ask because I know you will, there have been a couple of instances, but fortunately no fatalities thus far. Once a clipboard from someone's hand ended up on the ledge, but was retrieved, as were two students on separate occasions. They were close calls, with the students, but they both lucked out and the window was open so that they fell inward."

"But what about Maxwell?" Franley asked.

"The location in the theater that sometimes sends things off is also a sort of ledge," Yoshi said, sidestepping the inquiry about Maxwell.

"A beam," said Franley. "It's a beam. Just like the voice in the car said. *We all see the beams.*"

"Yes," said Alicia. "It's a beam on the catwalk."

"The catwalk! Why did we not break down the house doors? Why did we waste time wandering around bathrooms, if Maxwell may be in danger in there?" cried Franley. "And what, you just step on the beam of the catwalk and teleport?"

"Well, I guess you could call it that, but it seems less science fiction and more shifty," said Yoshi. "And you don't step on it. You touch it with your hands. There is a board, or beam on each side of the catwalk that is purposed as a handrail. One board is painted black, and one is painted silver. If you touch the silver one, the odds of you ending up at the Inventes is greater. Nothing has ever left by touching the black one. It would seem simple enough not to touch the silver one, but it is a challenge as the catwalk is not very wide and has been known to tilt."

"You were not joking about the safety codes," Franley replied. "Did no one ever think to fix it, or remove the beam, or just do anything about it? How often does this shifting, teleportation thing happen? Did it happen before the last time you all were here? Did it happen before they painted them? Am I now an accessory if I sell this place without warning people that there's a severely odd danger?"

The questions flooded out, her voice rising and falling as she realized her volume caused the shadow tendril to come to the edge of the door.

"The only tilting we ever experienced was when the house shifted on Mortimer and me, as you read in his story," Alicia replied in a steady quietness. "Everything else happened after. Most people don't really acknowledge that it has happened. Maxwell knows about it because he's been at the scene of—"

"Wait. You know Maxwell? Personally? It didn't seem like it when he came to the car," Franley interrupted.

"We don't know him personally. We just know that he knows. His cousin was one of the students that ended up going from here to there."

Franley didn't know what else to say. She felt blindsided. Here she had been thinking she had finally met people she could trust, people who were like her, but now she was learning they had been withholding serious information. She ran to each of the house doors and pushed against them, trying, hoping to break through. They did not give way. Slumping against the last one, she surveyed this couple before her; Alicia still gripping the sofa, Yoshi looking lost, the oval window looming high above them.

"Can I trust you?" she asked.

"Yes," Yoshi replied.

"We didn't tell you because it is a little weirder than the other things," Alicia said. "Even the two people who have survived the experience don't really know what to do with it."

"Who would? Is it really any weirder than you having experienced the same moment three times consecutively?" Franley pinged at Yoshi.

He shrugged in reply and said, "Guess not."

Alicia's phone vibrated and lit her pocket. While they waited for her to read the text, Franley caught Yoshi's eye and motioned her head toward the closed hall door from which they had fled.

"What is in there?"

"I don't really know any more than you do," he replied. "Really, I don't."

The look on her face did not convince him of her acceptance.

"Louisa says there are lights on in the room where the theater sends people. She tried to call the room by way of contacting the front desk, but no one at the desk answered." Alicia put her phone back in her pocket.

"Well, it's a hotel, right? Wouldn't it be normal for lights to be on in that room?" Franley asked.

"They try not to book that one, but it can happen when they are full, which they seem to be judging by Louisa's description of the parking lot." Alicia stood up.

"Wait. So, people do or do not acknowledge this *thing* happens? I mean wouldn't they just always book the room if they didn't believe in it? And if this town is so lacking by the descriptions you allude to in budgets etcetera, why would the hotel ever even be full?"

Franley was hot. She was angry and growing angrier by the second. The burn of it inflated and sweltered under every other emotion that swam about her. And yet, she knew it wasn't entirely *her* anger. It was also coming from elsewhere, being fueled from outside of herself, and she knew enough to know that she needed to gather herself, her actual self, and stop this intrusion of seething revulsion.

"Not everything is simple," Alicia replied. "The hotel does have some nice event space. Louisa is watching the window ledge from their atrium, which is one of their nicer features. They want to host groups and keep their heads monetarily above water the same as anyone. It's not like we are crazy far from places that do have interesting things to do and see and there's always the history aspect of our area."

Franley sighed, "I just—I don't feel right. Can we get Maxwell and go?"

"Do you want to step outside? Get some air?" Yoshi asked motioning to the doors leading out to the parking lot.

Franley looked at the doors to the outside and realized that she could not remember any of them having closed those doors, yet they were closed now. The playbills for Macbeth were neatly stacked back in the chair. She shook her head. For a moment, a brief fleeting moment, a man-sized shadow crossed in front of the doors. Once past them, it was no longer visible. She wanted to leave, but she could not bring herself to do so.

THE CONSEQUENT

Louisa wrestled with her indecision. Staring up at the window ledge, praying that no one would appear, she warred with her inner monologue. The desk had been so crowded upon her arrival that she had not been able to speak with anyone about the occupancy of the room. It was conceivable that they would not have shared any information with her despite her pleas. Afraid that there was no time to waste standing around the lobby, waiting or arguing, she had gone straight to the atrium. Now, she wondered if she should have gone straight to the elevators, or stairs instead. Perhaps she should have gone straight to room 400 and pounded on the door.

It was too late now. Her decision had been made. She could not retreat because there was too much distance and too much potential for what disasters could happen in the amount of time it would take to get from her current spot in the atrium to the door of 400. Relegating herself to a bench, she stared at the window up on the fourth-floor corner and wondered how she might get the attention of the occupant.

The flashlight of her phone would not shine far enough to be of any consequence. The only rocks in the atrium were large, well-polished things that would sail easily enough with her pitcher's arm but would also sail on through the glass and potentially harm whomever was on the other side. She had once sliced a teammate's forehead open with a leather mitt she had thrown at her from a short distance. The stitching of the mitt had caught at just the right angle and done enough damage to require stitches in the girl's forehead. She was pretty sure it had left a scar. That had been when she was twelve and playing little league with not so little dreams. Now she was far past twelve and dreaming only that maybe she would wake up and find that this town and her life had not become so strange.

It had been many years since she last threw anything and at that time she had thrown slightly smaller rocks than the ones here in the atrium. They had come from the alleyway next to the theater and she had been attempting to break the side windows. Though they were jagged and uneven the rocks bounced off those windows as if they were no heavier than toy putty. She had been frantic and afraid, and the rocks had turned into illusions in her hands.

Interlude

November 30, 2022 / August 03, 1991

There was thunder within and rain of torrential consequence. Hamish held the simple white sheets in a grip that camouflaged his knuckles with the linens. It had been a long time since the last incident. It had been so long that he thought it was behind him and perhaps if he had continued on without ever having another incident, he would have come to believe that it had all been a very bad dream.

Once upon a time Hamish had been a little boy. He had been a very careful, logical, and well-behaved child who did not enjoy fairytales, or ghost stories, or anything at all that was made up. The only inventions that interested him as a boy had been things that he could take apart, which was something he did often, and he always managed to put them back together. Sometimes the things he took apart were even better after he had reassembled them. His talents did not go unnoticed by his family. It was hard not to witness the regular dissection of items like the toaster, various alarm clocks, and the fancy vacuum cleaner his mother had saved up for. There was always a grateful appreciation when these items were put back together.

All of this went sideways and out the proverbial window when Hamish was only eight years old. When he was eight years old, a thing occurred that sent him down a different path from the one he had been following. Perhaps he may have grown up to be a mechanic, or an engineer, or a rocket scientist, or all of the above. Instead he had grown up to be in the sales business of formal attire and dabbled in event planning because controlling the look of things had appealed to him massively.

It was not something he considered on a regular basis and in fact he had mostly either forgotten or never realized why he went down the career path he had. Now, sitting in the dark of his hotel room, everything fell back into place. His life assembled piece by piece before him with the result being this fear soaked, well-dressed, well-groomed man sitting in a hotel room far from home, afraid to move and afraid to call out.

On the night of his eighth birthday, Hamish had gotten into bed all by himself. He had told his parents goodnight in the kitchen and bid them not to come upstairs because he felt, logically, he was now old enough to tuck himself in. He kissed his mother on the forehead, shook his father's hand, climbed the stairs, and calmly slipped under the soft green quilt on his bed. He had thought to himself that his parents had taken it very well, his growing up, and that he was proud of them for understanding, even if his father did seem to be stifling an amused sort of smile.

Hamish was just about to fall asleep when he saw a thing in the shadows on the top of his wardrobe that he did not remember being there before. It was dark in the room with only a little light filtering in from a small lamp in the hall. The thing was dark and shaped unlike any of the items so carefully arranged on the top of the wardrobe. In fact there had only been three items up there; a large teddy bear with a bow tie, a shoebox of cards collected from various birthdays and holidays, and a metal airplane he had assembled, and hand painted yellow.

This fourth thing that did not belong was not shaped like any of the items that Hamish knew to be there. If this new thing was shaped like anything his eight-year-old mind would recognize, it was shaped like a gumdrop he had accidentally melted when he dropped it over a lit gas stove. This thing, however, was much larger than a gumdrop, about the size of the large teddy bear and for a moment he began to see it as being so like the bear in size that he tossed around the idea that maybe his parents had gotten him another and placed it up on the wardrobe to see if he would notice. Today had been his birthday, so perhaps it was something like that, a gift, a surprise.

He sat up in bed and stared at the new shape, unafraid because he really had no reason to suspect there was anything sinister about this new development. This was just a new puzzle to solve, and he felt sure the most likely outcome would be a slightly late birthday present. With it being not quite shaped like the bear, but so similar in height, he settled on the idea of it being a cow. A stuffed toy cow would make sense because he was rather fond of them and when he was a toddler his aunt had called him *Little Moo* because he always picked out clothes in black and white. Perhaps his aunt had sent this toy cow. He was so sure it was indeed a cow and the more he thought about it the more he was sure it had been sent by his aunt and placed atop the dresser by his parents as a surprise.

Then it shifted. The shape slid and slouched. What Hamish had thought was the cow's front leg, now hung down the side of the wardrobe and no longer resembled a leg at all. It was too dense, thickly dark, and oddly almost one dimensional. Like a shadow plucked from the wall and moved forward into the air, this new shape fell from the dresser onto his floor. Rather it floated, but that wasn't really the right term for it either. It just moved. It moved from the top of the wardrobe onto the floor and Hamish had frozen with the inexplicableness of it. It remained on the floor for what seemed a very long time before it crawled like a rounded one-dimensional caterpillar to the bed and under it.

Until this moment, Hamish had not been able to move, or to speak. He had not been sure if he should be afraid, or if just being unsettled was okay. Now though, he screamed like he could not ever remember screaming before.

His parents came clambering up the stairs and down the hall, burst into his room, and threw on his light. He yelled at them, *Stop! Be careful! It's under the bed!*

Of course, they found nothing. Both mortified and embarrassed, though he knew it was real, he pleaded with them to take him out of his room. Surely, it was real. Surely, it had not been a dream. They conveyed it was a perk of his overactive child's imagination, offered him some water, and impressed upon him that all would be well if he just went to sleep.

Over the course of the next five years, Hamish would see this new shape that became the old familiar shape, over and over again. He would see it when he was awake. He would see it in his dreams. He even saw it at school once, though almost always it was in his room, atop his wardrobe. The antics the shape expressed were varied, but always unsettling.

After a year of calling out for his parents whenever he saw it and always being denied credibility, he took to taking instantly printable pictures of it, which never turned out, but always broke his camera until he got tired of fixing it and gave up taking pictures all together. How could a picture of anything ever be reliable if what he could plainly see with his eyes was not being captured by the mechanism and film? Giving up fixing his camera led to his giving up fixing other things and he no longer called out for help. What was the purpose in taking anything apart if there were things that defied structure and explainability?

One day his aunt, who called him *Little Moo,* asked why he wouldn't try to fix her radio that she had been nudging him about over the phone for a week before his family arrived to visit her. He simply told her that his eyes couldn't be trusted anymore. He wanted to say that his spirit gut could be trusted, but that seemed silly to say aloud, and he wasn't sure if his spirit gut knew how to fix radios.

Spirit gut was his new phrase for that feeling he got when he knew the shape was around. Sometimes he felt the shape in his spirit gut long before he ever saw it and sometimes, he didn't even see it at all, though he might see something in his presence being moved like the time his shoebox of cards had slid and toppled off the wardrobe and a card reading *SUPER FUN BIRTHDAY BOY* had spun out of the mess and landed at his feet.

His family moved when he was thirteen and his spirit gut had felt relieved. The visitations and manifestations had ceased. Here in the bed, in room 400 at Inventes, his spirit gut was screaming. Desperately, he wanted to call out, but there was no one to call out to. He would only frighten the other guests. He imagined the sound that would emanate from himself. It would be long, stretched, ankled, a deep throaty cry. If he had dared to move and reach for his phone, who would he dial? There was no one home. There hadn't been anyone waiting there for a long time. When he stopped calling out as a child for his parents, he had stopped asking for help altogether. There wasn't a singular time he could remember asking anyone for help. He had built his business from the ground up and he had done it alone. He had built no relationships because that seemed unnecessary and pointless, but he had forgotten to wonder why he felt this way. Now he knew. He remembered everything.

ACT II

Chapter 8

November 30, 2022

Franley watched as Yoshi opened the box office door. They hadn't looked there yet because it had seemed empty when they were in the parking lot and deciding to enter the theater.

"He's not here," Yoshi called back to them, looking in and glancing under the ticket desk. He closed the door and returned to the center of the lobby.

"Where to next?" asked Franley, eyeing the door to the house where when visiting with Dugan, he had asked her to follow, but where she had not been able to go. Now she was ready, but apparently not allowed.

"The right, around by the office," Alicia said, taking a step in that direction without waiting for affirmation from the others.

They followed her through the door to the right and down a hall that immediately turned toward the back of the theater. The lights here were overhead fluorescent and rather harsh compared to the rose and ivy lamps in the coat and restroom hall. Alicia had flipped them on hastily in the same moment she had swung the door open.

The whole of this hall was painted a flat grayish white. The only thing adorning the walls was a single oil portrait with a muddled backdrop that could have been a forest, a thick curtain, or the recesses of a nebula. The woman subjected within was clad with a flowing skirt of a pale lavender, so pale it was nearly gray. Her torso was lifted with a silver bodice, laced with a black cord. Her hair hung in soft blonde waves about her neck, and her eyes were painted so that the pools of black representing her pupils met your gaze from whichever way you stood. As such, she watched them walk down the hall.

They approached a closed door about halfway down with the word *Office* engraved on a silver plaque in the middle. Alicia spoke without looking back.

"Don't stop there. Keep going," she said quietly and quickly added, "Don't ask me now."

Neither Yoshi nor Franley said a word. They just kept moving forward behind her. When they reached the end of the hall there was a small quiet thump from behind them. Franley turned to see the office door that had been closed, slightly swaying out from the inner wall. A faint blue light lay on the carpet. Perceptibly, though barely, it fizzled and blinked. For a moment Franley thought about investigating, but heeding Alicia's warning and remembering the swaying light from the basement on Pin Row, she decided against it, though it had long troubled her that she had never gone back to that house and its secrets. Someone should investigate that basement—archaeologists, historians, the police. That light had not been blue like this one. It had looked and felt different entirely, but both beckoned.

Yoshi caught Franley's eye, as he too had turned to look. Then Alicia pushed open the door to the backstage area and ushered them onward as she held it open. Both saw her looking back before she closed her eyes in a silent prayer, letting the door close behind.

Alicia had seen what was in the office, not with her eyes and not in her mind, but in some inner space that lingered just outside of her mind and somehow spoke into it. This was the way she had tried to describe it to Yoshi on the night she had first gotten permission from Louisa to investigate the theater, when she had invited him to come along. It had been told differently to Mortimer back then and unfortunately, the lie of it was perpetuated unknowingly by him into the archives of Imagine

Shadows. There had never been a medium at her suggestion. It had only been her, Louisa, and Yoshi.

Alicia did not consider herself a medium and had never really thought of herself as one in training as had been stated in Mortimer's submission. She had always known she had abilities, but she did not understand them very well in her younger years. Now, she was more comfortable with them, but still aware that she did not have the capacity to fully understand how it all worked.

Perhaps the confusion of her being a medium in training began before the lie. She had tried to raise the subject of the supernatural a few times at rehearsals because she wanted to know if she was alone in seeing what she saw. The shadowed man in the third to last row, in the fourth seat from the end, nearest the side aisle and wall was the only entity she had witnessed there in the years leading up to her investigation. He occurred so often that she had become quite used to him, though he had startled her quite enough when she came in late with Louisa and Yoshi, causing her to scream from sheer surprise, and thereby startling Louisa into a door frame. That evening had been so different from what she had expected, but it would not be until the evening the theater was sold that she would come to harbor fear and regret. The fear was not so much for what the theater contained, but for feeling she had endangered her closest friends and yet selfishly not wanted to let go of the place. It was true that she had not wanted Louisa to sell it, not initially, though she had been quick to change her mind. In addition to the horror of having endangered others with her carelessness, there too was the shame for lying to Mortimer and for coercing Louisa and Yoshi into taking part, hoping to avoid his disdain. Despite all that he and she had shared on the very last night when they had been locked into the house together, she had never divulged the truth to him and after that experience she had been glad to let the theater go.

Shame, she thought, was a nasty burden to bear. She couldn't even remember why she had believed Mortimer needed to think there was an outside medium who came in. What possibly could have been the difference between her suggesting one versus being one? But she wasn't one.

She told herself this over and over. She was not a medium. A medium, she thought, was someone who actively tried consulting the dead, or *something,* and in the worst cases simply fooled mourners into believing their loved ones were sending them well wishes. Some were tricksters, or at minimum well-meaning people who themselves were being fooled. She did not function like that. What happened to Alicia just happened—*except* for the one time, the evening when she investigated the theater, after months of begging Louisa for the chance. Feeling bold and brave and as if she may finally find a use for her talents, she had been played. The one and only time she had used a tool other than herself, a naïve child so sure of discovering a new world, she chose a talking board and allowed the theater to access her as the outlet for what it had wanted to say.

The board was homemade. Alicia had thought it would be best to make it herself to avoid any pre-contamination from previous use or imbuing of the materials by some ill-meaning seller. It was a sanded down slice of oak from a stump in the front lot of her apartment complex that she had resided in at the time. She sliced it herself, ignoring the inquisitive glances from the neighbors. She chose the stump because it was circular and she knew that she would be using it alone, not with others joining together in a circle, so it seemed a positive thing for the board itself to be round. The danger of the endeavor was not lost on her, but with the proper precautions and extra care, she believed it would be minimal.

The evening before she went to investigate, she hand painted the alphabet and numbers zero to nine in two concentric circles on the top of the oak slab. The numbers were the inner ring, and she added the words 'yes' and 'no' to the center, with the word good-bye below them. Good-bye was a little smaller than she would have liked, but she figured she could plan better for the next board she made. She didn't know it then, but she would never be using or making a talking board again. Things had not gone well, but she could not dwell on that now.

Opening her eyes, from her prayer and the memories that danced behind it, asking God for protection and forgiveness, Alicia stared out at the backstage area and reached for Yoshi's hand. The darkness was offset just slightly by windows to the right, that looked out into the side alley. She smiled, remembering how her friends had tried to break one of the windows when she and Mortimer had been trapped inside. Louisa had later admitted that the bigger rocks they had found and thrown from the gravel lot had merely bounced back at them, as if the windows were not glass at all, but something buoyant like rubber.

Her smile faded quickly, as Franley had begun to move ahead without them. She was headed for a door at the back wall, about three yards in front. Her phone had been drawn from her purse, and she had turned the flashlight on.

Pulling herself fully back into the present, Alicia called out, "Franley, wait!" She grabbed Yoshi by the hand and ushered him along with her as she moved toward Franley.

"I'm out," Franley said. "I should've left earlier. Whatever was back there—I'm just—I'm out. Now."

"That's not really an exit," Yoshi called.

Franley halted and spun toward them. "What do you mean it isn't an exit?" She gestured with her phone light to the sign over the back door. "Looks like it says, 'EXIT'." She resumed her march toward it.

"It just goes into a narrow hallway and then a staircase that only goes up. It leads to the apartments in the back half of the building," Alicia said.

Franley ran to the door and threw her shoulder against it. It begrudgingly opened into a narrow hall more barren than the one they had come from before entering the backstage area. It was without light, though she could faintly make out a staircase at the end. She stepped back and let the door shut with a quiet thud.

"You okay, Franley?" asked Yoshi. He tightened his grip on Alicia's hand.

"I shouldn't be here," she said. "I promised my kids French toast in the morning, and I was supposed to be back to tuck them in, and then I was supposed to open a bottle of wine with Bill. That bottle has been sitting in the fridge for three months."

"They seemed understanding earlier when we talked to them in the car," Yoshi offered.

"They are understanding. Liza, my youngest, thinks that I'm a grand adventurer and Billy thinks, well I don't know what he thinks, not really. He just imitates whatever Bill says and Bill plays the role of supporter quite well. So, naturally Billy does too, at least on the surface. I shouldn't be here. I shouldn't be here in this nonsense construction of a place with whatever else is here. I'm not fooling anyone. This isn't my job. It's not about my job. I just wanted to know, to understand, and to get Maxwell to safety, but I really need to leave now."

Franley moved past them, still shining her phone light into her path. "Is there another exit on the other side of this backstage area?"

"It just leads into the house," Alicia said.

"Of course it does," Franley replied.

"You can go back the way we came. I think it will be okay."

"You think? You mean you don't *know*?" Franley stammered, catching sight of Alicia's face in the darkness. "I'm sorry. I am just–I'm not sure what's wrong with me in here."

"It's okay," Alicia said. "We will walk you back to the front. I'll message Louisa and maybe we can get someone else more official to look for Maxwell." Hearing Franley confess wanting to know, to understand, was a resonant reminder of her own past mistake and maybe tonight was a mistake too. She didn't really want to go back past the office, but it seemed better than going through the house.

Franley nodded and pushed on the door to go back into the hall they had come from. The door wouldn't budge. For a moment she thought she must be doing it wrong and looked for a handle to pull on, but there wasn't one.

"It won't open," she whispered.

Yoshi let go of Alicia's hand and pushed on the door with Franley. The door remained fixed.

"It's okay, we could just cut through the apartment side of the building. It'll be a longer walk back to the front down the alleyway, but I think some night air would be a good change," he said, moving away from the door.

"There's an exit from the second floor at the back of the building, down a staircase in that hall."

So, it is an exit, Franley thought. Rolling her eyes, she tried to suppress the rising swell of anger that was pushing itself to the surface. However, it did not matter if that route had been an exit as that door would no longer open either.

Chapter 9

November 30, 2022

Holding the phone light in front of her with one hand, Franley adjusted the strap of her purse across her shoulder and smoothed her hand over the front flap, letting it rest there for a moment. She thought about what a long entry this night was going to make and about how there wasn't much room left on the long sheet of yellow paper she had used to create her list. How many pages would she fill in her lifetime? She hoped there would be a lot of life pages but not necessarily filled with these types of experiences. Still, there was no getting away from this one. There was no turning back. Whoever was wandering this building with them had made sure of it. They would check backstage, which by the scarce look that she could garner through the phone light, did not seem like it would take long. They would then hopefully find their way into the house, and back out to the lobby, and with any luck locate poor Maxwell along the way.

"Maxwell?" Yoshi called out. "Maxwell? Buddy if you're back here, now would be a good time to come on out."

"We can check the dressing rooms. There's two around the corner," Alicia offered, not even glancing back at the doors that would not open.

They moved through the dark, side by side, with the light of Franley's phone. Franley wondered why neither of the others bothered to take theirs out for extra lighting, or why no one was going for a light switch, but in her growing discomfort and agitation, she said nothing. She just wanted to get on with it and get out.

There was a rustle to their left and Franley thought she saw dark curtains move in the small panel window of a door that she surmised must lead to the stage left wing. Again she said nothing but kept moving forward. Dark shapes loomed everywhere. Props, drop cloths, bins, and carts holding various boxes that may have housed light bulbs, or microphones, or makeup were stacked and haphazardly scattered about. Franley tried to occupy herself with guessing the contents. Whatever was in the boxes could be fun, normal, mundane.

"I don't remember it being this cluttered before," Yoshi said.

"Louisa would have never let us keep it this way," Alicia replied with a touch of fondness.

"Have you heard from her recently?" asked Franley.

"No, but I'm sure she'll reach out, if she sees anything, or gets ahold of anyone," Alicia responded. "The dressing rooms are over there by the stage right entrance, just across from it."

Having navigated their way through the clutter of the university student's past performances, they came around the other side of the room. There were two doors off to the right, as Alicia had said. Franley thought they looked like closet doors and snorted aloud as she thought to herself of finding skeletons in them.

"What for?" asked Alicia.

"Just thinking it would be funny if we found a skeleton in the closet," Franley answered.

"Well, those are the dressing rooms. Hopefully, they are void of anything other than costumes."

Franley wasn't sure if Alicia sounded mad, or tired. She was sure that she herself was both.

They opened the ladies' dressing room first. Rows of dresses poured out of the recesses in the form of thick shapes, tattered, and dense against the sides of each wall. A frosted window at the back of the room cast yellow light from a streetlamp outside, reminding Franley of the frosted dandelion glass on the post office house at Pin Row. It was both off putting and comforting. At least there was a familiarity to it and a sign of life beyond this building.

"Maxwell?" Yoshi called out again.

No one moved to enter the room. They backed up instead and left the door open. The light of the streetlamp did nothing to illuminate the space they stood in. Opening the door to the men's dressing room, Yoshi called out for Maxwell once more. Once more, there was no reply. Another frosted window glowed yellow from the back. The side walls were lined here too with what Franley assumed were costumes. Assumptions were a dangerous game at any time, but in this place, she did not want to guess what else the shapes may be.

Under the window was a desk chair, wooden, with a fabric seat that may have been red, or purple, or black. It was impossible to be sure in this light. It was angled toward the window and then it wasn't. With a tilt, it balanced on its back legs for a few seconds and then dropped to the floor with a clatter that made them jump even though each had been holding their breath in anticipation of the inevitable tumble. Collectively, they took a step away from the men's dressing room, as Yoshi shut the door. In the light of Franley's phone, his face held the singular expression of one who was completely done.

He turned and looked Alicia full on. "Maxwell may not even be in the building anymore. He may have walked out. He probably cut through the apartments."

She said nothing in return. She simply swung her head to face the side wing entrance for performers and crew entering stage right.

"Do we take stage and check for him in the wings, or just walk out into the house?" Yoshi continued.

"I think we want to get out of here, preferably now. I know I would like that," Franley offered. "So, I'm taking the door to the house."

"You'll be coming in on his side," Alicia said, walking over to the door Franley was also headed for. Alicia got there first and peered through a small square window. "He's already waiting," she said.

No explanation was given and none was required. Franley and Yoshi knew what she meant. Each paused in their own summation of what this statement held. Each wondered in silence if this had been his doing all along, calling them in with the lights, sealing the doors behind them, routing them to this exact spot, leaving them with two options—either they took stage, or they took a seat in the audience. Even if the doors at the house entrance into the lobby were open, would it be rude, or unkind to leave at present? Each wondered in silence why they themselves were concerned about manners.

Franley's phone vibrated in her hand. She flipped off the flashlight and turned the screen to read a rambling message from Dugan.

You would make a wonderful renovator, Franley. Don't you like what I've done with the place? Updated lighting can make all the difference. Don't you think? I've been dreaming again, across the sea.

She thought about replying and telling him what they could see through the small window on the door, asking him what exactly it was that he had done, and telling him off for playing with her emotions at exactly the wrong time, but then she decided there was no need. He must already know, and she must not let him anger her. This odd man had sent her unhinged texts before, but she had shrugged them off as the ramblings of an eccentric. He had, however, never sent words of her exact whereabouts. *Dreaming again. Dreaming again.* This place had quite the reach. She held the phone out for the others to see and read.

"He used to dream about this place," Alicia said. "Before he ever came here, he dreamt of it."

Franley remembered this from Mortimer's story. She was glad to find it was true, even if it was unsettling, at least it was true. Even if things were about to go sideways, it was a thread to hold onto.

"He has a connection to the piano, or this place. We don't really understand," Alicia added.

"It's unhealthy," Yoshi said.

"Doubt it."

They all looked at one another. The skin on Franley's arms rippled with a crawling sensation under her black denim sleeves. She could see in the others' eyes that they had heard it too. Yoshi turned to Alicia, searching her for a sign of understanding.

"I don't know," she whispered. "I think... I think it's not the good one."

Franley shot her a look. The anger that she had been working to suppress had been flitting around, more subdued in the back of her chest. Now it rose to her throat.

Yoshi grabbed Alicia's arm and bent his head close to hers. "The small one?" he whispered.

"The child who is not a child," she whispered back.

"Doubt it!" The voice giggled and the door to the stage wing slammed.

None of them had seen it open. A loud thwack came from behind them, from behind the closed door to the men's dressing room. *Thwack. Thwack. Thwack.* The pounding came as if someone were throwing the chair against the door in rapid succession.

"We should just go through the house, manners be damned," Yoshi said motioning for them to follow. Alicia reached out and put her hand on his shoulder.

Franley, already alarmed beyond what she had ever experienced, even beyond the encounter with Oscar, yelled out, "Manners? Why did you say that? What is wrong with you? Why are you inside my head!"

"Franley, it's not us and you know it. Be quiet and keep moving," Yoshi replied.

The anger in her throat shot down and out through her shoulders and arms. She shoved him, knocking Alicia free of her grip on him. He stumbled forward, catching himself just before the door. Turning back to her, he opened his mouth with a harsh breath. Alicia put her hand out in a motion to stop. Then she put her other hand on Franley and began to pray. She said the words internally, but Yoshi saw what she was doing and held his tongue. Franley stood there, not sure what to do. She was suddenly, extremely, taken aback by this rage.

She knew this emotion was not coming from her. It was rioting under her skin. This building anxiety and funneling of fear was something she had never experienced before, not at this level. With Alicia praying over her, it began to dwindle and lessen, but she could still feel it prickling on the insides of her skin. All over her body it felt as if each nerve ending held a series of tiny nerve endings within and she could not be master of them all. Closing her eyes, she focused and prayed to God for discernment over this anger and she prayed she could trust Alicia and if she could trust her, that whatever it was Alicia was praying over her, would come to fruition and that soon they could all go home.

Franley whispered, "*Holy, holy, holy is the Lord God Almighty who was and who is and who is to come,*" and Alicia and Yoshi joined in and together they repeated it once more.

Chapter 10

The night Louisa had let Alicia investigate the theater was three months prior to the day the university had come for the one act and tour, and thus three months prior to the day the theater had given Mortimer and Alicia the performance of a lifetime.

Yoshi had joined them at her invitation. Alicia had thought it was for the purpose of spending more time with her. That was true in part, but it turned out that he also wanted to know more about the place, the shadowed man, and the potential opportunity to get a glimpse into the composition of time by way of ghosts. She didn't yet know his story about the time recycle when he was fifteen, when he had lived the same moment three times consecutively. He would tell her eventually, but on this night, he remained oddly silent, even for his usually reserved manner.

She had shrugged it off as nerves. Wielding a talking board in a haunted building wasn't something that most people could be relaxed about, and she hadn't exactly told anyone that she would be bringing it. Louisa had asked a few questions when she saw it but had refused to touch it when Alicia had extended it out for examination. Yoshi had merely walked away and stood looking up at the stained-glass oval window in the lobby.

When Louisa excused herself for a moment, promising they would get started shortly, Alicia had walked over and intentionally bumped into Yoshi who remained fixed to his spot, arms folded, eyes up.

"Seems like the designer forgot to add charm or whimsy," Alica said, looking up at the window too.

Yoshi tilted his head as if he were about to speak but changed his mind. He smiled slightly.

They stood staring for a few moments before Alicia noticed for the first time that the black iron, outer frame of the window and the bar that ran across the center were one piece. She had looked at it so many times without observing it and said as much to Yoshi. His reply was, "It's a little different around the edges, the glass coloration."

Alicia noted that perhaps it was. Louisa popped back into the room with a heavy-duty flashlight.

"I think it's time," she said.

"Yes," replied Yoshi.

Alicia and Yoshi settled in the middle of the stage. Louisa stood in the wings, watching and wondering silently to herself if she was about to get a show, or an answer. She hoped for an answer. All the lights in the house were on. The board sat between Alicia and Yoshi who sat cross-legged on either side and angled so that Alicia could see out into the house. Yoshi was positioned so that he was facing toward the back curtain, but also so that Louisa could see the board from the side, so that he would not be blocking her view.

"Have you used one of these before?" he asked, watching Alicia take a few deep breaths and stretch her arms out in a warmup of sorts. She smiled and shook her head.

"Well, this one looks nice. You did a nice job on it." He meant that. He also didn't expect anything to happen. There was something going on here, he believed that much, but he did not expect the board to be any more than a slumber party game that perhaps at its most proper working state, gave itself over to subconscious emotions.

"I was in the room with one at a slumber party once," she answered as if he had spoken aloud. "I didn't touch it while it was being used, but I did touch it the next morning. Just gave it a tap.

"What happened while it was being used?" Yoshi asked.

"It told another girl at the party that she had an admirer and that his name was Loxley."

"Did she? Was that a boy from school?"

"She didn't know anyone with that name and neither did we. We searched our yearbooks and the telephone book but couldn't come up with him."

"Maybe it was a misunderstanding." Yoshi smiled in jest.

"I don't think so. During the night, when everyone else was asleep, I saw the planchet move on its own accord and it spelled, *Loxley wants out.*"

Alicia frowned down at her board and missed the look of suppressed surprise on Yoshi's face.

"Are you sure?" he asked.

She was glancing around and feeling in her sweater pockets for something.

"Hm?" she answered in her distraction.

"Did it really move on its own? Did it really spell that?" Yoshi replied.

"Yes. I know what I saw, but I—I forgot a planchet. I didn't make one."

"Oh. Well, that's alright. What does it typically look like? Maybe we can find something in the prop closet, or the tool chest?"

"It looks like a rounded flower petal, or a guitar pick. Sometimes—" Alicia was going to say that it sometimes had a hole in the middle, but Yoshi had jumped up, shouting that he would be right back. She looked up at Louisa nervously fidgeting in the wings and waved. "I forgot a planchet."

Louisa forced a smile.

Yoshi returned a moment later, walking forward with tempered gusto and held out a small red guitar pick. "This will do?"

"That should be perfect." She took it from his outstretched hand. He thought he might melt when her fingertips met his, but stoically he sat himself back on the floor of the stage, checked his position with Louisa, and did his best to keep a straight face.

Alicia placed the pick in the center of the board above the yes and no, so that it wasn't pointing to anything specific. She gave Louisa a nod and began her attempt at communication.

"Hello. We extend an invitation of friendship and communication to whomever is here with us. If you are here with us and are willing to communicate with us, we invite you to move the guitar pick to spell out your reply."

The pick did not move.

"We ask that if you are here and are willing to communicate, that you will use this board to speak with us. We mean no disrespect and only wish to understand your presence. Will you communicate with us?"

A slam came from the back of the house, as if someone had opened the door to the lobby and slammed it behind them, despite the fact that the doors from the house to the lobby were incapable of making such a noise. The pick remained still.

"Did you see anything?" Yoshi whispered. Alicia shook her head no.

"We would like to get to know you. We are aware that you remain in this theater. Will you communicate with us?" she reached out again.

The pick did not move.

Are you supposed to touch the pick? Yoshi wanted to ask, but he did not want to interrupt again.

"I know the planchet, the pick, can be moved by you. Will you communicate with us, by moving the pick?"

The pick did not move.

Alicia glanced over at Louisa and back at the board. She knew there was someone here, aside from the slam of the door. She could sense someone hovering behind her and another someone standing or maybe kneeling off to the side.

She placed the pointer finger of her right hand onto the guitar pick. Immediately, the pick began to dart around the board in rapid criss crossing motions. Yoshi watched with all the restraint he could muster. *Surely, she'll stop this soon.*

For a full minute the pick darted around to letters and numbers without making any sense. It moved quickly without stopping on any of the hand painted symbols.

"Did you slam the door?" Alicia asked.

The pick stopped in the center on the word, **No.**

"Who slammed the door?"

The pick fidgeted for a moment under her finger like an insect caught beneath a window screen. Then it flew to the letter **M**, then to **A**, and then on to **N** where it rested.

Yoshi looked Alicia full in the eyes, searching for her truth. *Was she moving the pick?*

She met his gaze and shook her head.

"Who is the man?" she asked.

The pick quivered and moved back to the **M**, then to **A**, and then on to **N**. Then it moved back to the **M**, then to **A**, and then on to **N**.

Again and again. **M A N. M A N. M A N. M A N. M A N. M A N. M A N. M A N.**

"Okay. Okay," Alicia called out as the pick made to move back to the M again. "Thank you."

The pick stopped and rested back in the middle, pointing at nothing.

"Can you tell me who you are? Who am I speaking with?" she asked.

The pick moved to **B**, then to **A, K, E**, and rested on **R.**

"Is that your name?" Alicia tilted her head and watched as the pick moved to the **Yes** in the center of the board. "Is that your first name?"

The pick remained where it was. Alicia looked up at Yoshi and said, "I think that means it is."

Yoshi, who was biting his lip at this point, transfixed with what was happening, nodded in reply.

"That's a nice name. Are you a boy?" asked Alicia.

The pick stayed put.

"How old are you, Baker?"

The pick moved to the number 5.

"You are very young," Alicia said.

The pick zoomed back to the center and settled on **No**.

"Oh. I'm sorry," said Alicia. "Five is old enough to do lots of things."

Yes.

"What kinds of things do you like, Baker?"

P L A Y

"Me too. Playing is fun. So, are plays like what we perform. Which kind do you mean? Do you like to play, or do you like watching the plays?"

P L A Y

Y O U

"You want to play with me? Or do you like the plays that I am in?"

P L A Y

W I T H

Y O U

"I would like that. What would you like to play?"

Surely, she knows what she is doing, Yoshi thought, looking back at Louisa who was clutching the black, velvet curtains in the wings with an expression that repeated his thoughts.

The guitar pick quivered again, but did not move. The slamming of the house door rocked their attention to the back of the house, spinning their gaze toward it in unison. There was nothing to be seen.

"Is the man here?" Alicia asked.

The pick stopped quivering.

"Baker, is the man here?"

There was silence from the board, but the air around them began to jump as if suddenly the entire house had become a conduit for something unseen. The hairs on their arms rose with static lift and all the lights flickered at once. The lights doused all the way down and then shot back to full strength. This happened three times and then all went out. The slamming commenced again, as if each entrance into the house was being opened and closed with extravagant force, in unison, and palpable anger.

A single plink from the piano sounded and the lights came back on. Alicia and Yoshi were both looking down at where the board should be, but the board was gone. They turned to Louisa who frantically was pointing across the stage. They followed the direction of her gesture to find a lady in a silver muslin gown, edged with lace, stooping and motioning for a medium sized dog with tight curls of white hair, who was halfway between where they sat and who Alicia initially presumed was his mistress. In the dog's mouth was the board. He carried it away with a trot but refused to give it to the lady who had summoned him. He stopped before her, shook his head vigorously with the board clenched in his teeth, then turned, leapt from the stage, and bounded down the aisle to the sound booth where he walked through the wall and was gone from sight, as too was the lady in silver.

Louisa ran out onto the stage and grabbed hold of Alicia.

"I thought it was you. I thought, maybe it was you, moving the guitar pick, but it wasn't you. It really wasn't."

"No. No it wasn't me." Alicia gripped Louisa's arms. "It wasn't me." She was sweating, a wild gleam in her eyes. She broke into a giggle. "We saw them! We saw them! They were just as real and tangible as you and me! Yoshi, you saw them too, right?"

Yoshi was standing looking out at the place where the dog had vanished into the sound booth wall. He did not reply for several moments.

"What will we tell the others?" he said when he finally spoke.

"The truth," replied Alicia with enthusiasm she intended to be contagious.

"What is the truth?" he asked.

"What do you mean? What we saw. What we saw is the truth. The guitar pick moving, the lady, the dog, the lights and the doors," Alicia replied with giddy abandon, still clutching Lousia's arms.

"Why did the guitar pick only move when you touched it? You said you had seen a planchet move on its own. Why did you have to touch it?" Yoshi turned to face them.

"Do you not believe me, or do you not believe yourself?" Alicia asked, trying not to yell.

"I just want to understand," he sighed.

"I didn't move it. I think Baker needed my energy."

Yoshi frowned and took a step toward them. Louisa and Alicia let loose their grip on each other.

"The one I saw as a kid, I think it moved on its own because of all the emotion and energy we had poured into the room and maybe what the other girls had poured into the board."

"In—into the board?" Yoshi stammered.

"Yes. We were excitable little girls, and we poured out energy and the board kept it. Maybe. I don't really know, but I know that's what I saw." Alicia was growing more flustered. How could he not see what an amazing thing had just happened? Why must he question everything so diligently?

"So, tonight, you let someone that you don't know, that you cannot see—you let that thing use you?" Yoshi began to bite his lips again.

"Well, yes. I guess I did. It worked though, didn't it? And it wasn't a thing!" Alicia threw her hands up.

Yoshi turned to Louisa pleading. "Louisa, tell me you understand what I'm getting at. Tell me this whole event didn't seem dangerous. How do we know that Baker is a five-year-old boy? Is there a history of a five-year-old boy with that name here? If there is, how do we know this isn't just some imposter taking advantage of our emotions? Tell me what you believe. Tell me I'm not wrong."

Louisa wavered for a moment, looking from one to the other, and then straightened herself up and said, "I don't know what to think, but I know what I saw. I think maybe the dog is a good being and the lady is maybe a good being and the rest, well the rest, I don't know."

Alicia and Yoshi stared at each other in silence.

"It's time to lock up and head out for the night. I think we all need some space to break this down in our own ways," Lousia said, bending down to pick up what lay in the gap between them.

She stood up with the red guitar pick in her fingers. "Put this back where you found—" her voice trailed off as her eyes fell upon the shadowed man in the third to last row, in the fourth seat from the end, nearest the side aisle and wall. The others followed her gaze. No one spoke, but they all wondered the same thing. Had he been enjoying the events playing out upon the stage, the aftermath of their investigation? Was he a friend or a foe or neither, but some other reality just outside of reach?

They quietly moved off stage, down the side steps into the opposite side of the house from where he sat. Once down from the stage they did not look over toward the shadowed man. They hurriedly walked up the side aisle to the doors. Alicia was in front with Louisa directly behind her, closely followed by Yoshi. Alicia pushed the door open toward the lobby. The shadowed man stood directly before her. She screamed with such urgency and pitch that Lousia slammed into the door frame in her haste to flee the other way. In a blink, he was gone. Without waiting another moment, they bolted past the lobby, leaving all the lights on behind them.

At different times after that, they would all look in the sound booth for the talking board, without ever mentioning such to each other until a couple months had passed. None of the three were ever able to locate it, or to understand how a solid board had passed through a solid wall in the mouth of a phantom dog.

Chapter 11

November 30, 2022

It did not seem so long ago when he had caught Alicia in the parking lot, held her with resolute compassion as she cried onto his chest, and then watched her dragged home by a friend who did not understand, but who simply felt that she must lie down and take off the crystal from around her neck, as if that had anything to do with what had happened to her and Mortimer.

Her remorse had been real and her growth exponential. The Alicia, Yoshi saw now, with her hand upon Franley and her prayers silent, but obvious, was the same woman he had always seen from day one. She hadn't been the same, but she had. It was like some unrealized portion of herself had yet to surface and yet he had been able to glimpse it through the tension and buoyancy of her being. Perhaps he had a way of *knowing* things too before they revealed themselves, at least with mortal people. Franley was alright, he could tell that much. She just needed to get out of this place. It was clear that her worries at home and her insecurities were a detriment to the oppressive game being played here in the theater. This was not a safe place for her to be. Whatever had been toying with them, was targeting her specifically and capitalizing on her weaknesses, making her more and more irritable. It was imperative they leave before it could harass her any further.

Alicia opened her eyes. "Franley," she said, "Franley, we need to move quickly. Whatever you see and whatever you hear, some of it will not be true."

"How will I know the difference?" Franley asked.

"Trust your instincts," Alicia said. Her stomach grumbled inopportunely, breaking the tension and alleviating some of Franley's nervousness.

"Trust my gut?" quipped Franley.

"Well, more like your spirit—your spirit gut, I guess you could say." Alicia's stomach grumbled again. She turned away shaking her head and motioned for Yoshi to open the door to the house when he was ready. Franley had known what Alicia meant when she said to trust her instincts, but there was relief in the broken tension. Whatever happened on the other side of the door, she was thankful to have these two looking out for her. If she had had any sense, she never would have come here and she never would have kept the listing after Dugan had brought her there for the first time. It didn't seem to matter though, whether she had any sense or not. These things found her, chased her, showed themselves, and wound their way to her door, proverbial or otherwise.

"I'm sorry I pushed you and I'm sorry you haven't had dinner yet," she whispered in their direction, but there was no reply because Yoshi had opened the door, and they had gone.

There was a blackness. The depth of such, Franley had never seen. There was a dense aura to the blackness that undulated, though she could not actually see the movement, as much as she could sense it. Calling out for the others did not feel advisable and perhaps was not possible. She was not even sure this color was black. It was perhaps too many colors and too few colors all at the same time, quivering and bolstering and pulsating.

She dared not move and she dared not stay standing where she was. Her left ear began to buzz with a high and flitting sound like a bugle being drowned in static and lightning, if lightning was a sound and not a visual. For reasons that she had no comprehension of, she leaned into that buzzing hum and followed it. She knew right then if she were ever to be asked about why she followed that sound she would have no answer other than it seemed like it had been the only call to make.

There were steps. She remembered seeing them and maneuvered up them from the same memory, impressed that she did not fall. At the top of the steps there was a door. She reached for the knob, but it was already open, and her hand waved out into emptiness, except it didn't actually seem to be emptiness because here she found she could see her hand and wrist. Stepping forward the visibility increased up her arm, drawing her gaze to her torso. She saw her black denim jacket ending at her waist, and the line of her skirt ending at her knees, and the boots on her feet down below where she ended, and the wooden floor began.

When she looked back up, the darkness had gone entirely, and she was in the wings staring at the strangest light she had ever seen. Opulently orange, with a glow that doused everything beyond the center of the stage into obscurity, it seemed strained like a lightbulb close to burning out.

In the center of the stage was a man seated on a chair. He turned, as if sensing that she was near, and called out to her.

"Mrs. Parker?"

Franley recognized the voice from their brief meeting earlier that night. She peered through the violent orange glow, trying to decipher the figure. She wanted to be sure it was him before she replied.

"Mrs. Parker?"

His voice was a little raspy, a little afraid. She thought the shirt he wore might have been blue, but it was so hard to tell in this awful light.

"Mrs. Parker, I hate to inform you. I must inform you. You understand, Mrs. Parker? I have to tell you."

The orange vibrated as if taking on his words and channeling them out in some visible frequency. They sunk in her stomach, hot stones she fought against. *This isn't real.*

"Mrs. Parker your husband is in the rafters."

She almost laughed. It was so positively obtuse and bizarre. Bill wasn't in the rafters. He was at home, probably even asleep by now and yet under her desire to laugh there was a dreadful sagging in her heart.

"You're not Maxwell," she whispered. "Nice try."

Turning to leave, little white paisley shapes flitted about her periphery, forcing her eyes to dart about and refocus on the center of the stage. The orange light quivered, and the little white paisley shapes unwhirled into many little white stripes, forming a funnel, forming a boy where the unreal Maxwell had been. The orange light was gone, and the chair was gone, as well. There was just a boy, about five years old. He was brightly white, but only for a moment, then he was tangible and real enough with messy blonde hair and white, untied sneakers.

"Daddy is in the rafters," he said with the saddest voice that sounded just like her son Billy, though she could not recall him ever sounding that sad. Clearly, this wasn't Billy. This boy did not even look like him and the sadness of this being's voice was not relayed in the eyes. His eyes gleamed sardonic, flickering with a faint and fleeting orangeness.

"Up there," he motioned. "Save my Daddy."

Looking upward, Franley saw there was indeed a man in the rafters, or on the catwalk rather. The catwalk was swaying, tilting just as Yoshi had said it would. The board painted black, and the board painted silver were indeed running along parallel sides of the catwalk and Yoshi wobbled in between them.

"Yoshi!" Franley called out. "Yoshi! Get low, bend down, and hold onto the floor. We'll get you down!"

Franley wasn't sure who 'we' was because Alicia was nowhere to be seen, but she had to get him down. It was her fault he was in here and now up there and she couldn't let him end up on a window ledge. She couldn't be the reason he didn't get to go home tonight. *Home. They should all be home.* Tentatively, she stepped out onto the stage, maneuvering around a floor stand with a single stage light attached.

136

"Up! Up! Up!" The boy giggled and bounced up and down on his white sneakers. "Up! Pick me up!" He stuck his tongue out at her and made an incomprehensible noise before he funneled back into a series of paisley stripes that ran gleefully off into the opposite wing.

The deep dark inkwell of blackness returned and overtook the stage.

"Yoshi! Can you hear me?" she called out. The darkness suffocating her words, cloying at her lungs. Her voice was barely audible. She tried again with a result that was only slightly louder. "Yoshi?"

She tried a third time.

"Alicia! Where are you?" It came out as a scream and echoed crushingly back off the swelling blackness. Tears forming in her eyes, she knelt down and felt the hardwood of the stage beneath her hands and a rougher texture that she recognized as masking tape. She had found her mark.

With this realization beneath her fingers the anger began to swell again. She did not want to be toyed with, played out, like a doll performing for this child who was not a child, or this shadowed man. She was sure he must be watching. She made to call out again to cast her tirade upon him and his presumed enjoyment of her situation, when from the blackness there came a familiar wafting. Cedary, leathery, strolling, and streaming, the scent of a cigar slipped across her face nearly stopping her heart.

How? How? How? Her pulse pummeled as if a slow anvil being lifted and brought back down by some strange gravity. *How? How? How?*

Waiting in the blackness for his hot breath, or the word *Pocket*, she tried not to think his name, as if that might summon into reality this unreal presentation. *Surely, it was not real.*

There was a hand on her back.

"Franley?"

The tears that had been forming, that she had been withholding, broke free. Her face fell to meet her hands at the floor. Huddled, sobbing, trembling, she felt the hand lift.

"Franley? What happened?"

A figure knelt before her and called again.

"Franley? What happened? Where's Yoshi?"

With frantic realization, Franley jolted up, her face damp and welted. Just barely seeing Alicia before her, she clamored to her feet. Looking up at the rafters, Franley began to run back and forth across the stage, searching, but to no avail. Yoshi was gone.

The Other Chapter 11

November 30, 2022

He opened the door and stepped out into the house. It fell away before him. He reached back to grab hold of Alicia, but she was not there, and neither was Franley. There was just a blackness the likes of which he had never seen. It ebbed and flowed and billowed with flecks of red and miniscule bursts of blue and he could not be sure if they were really part of the landscape, or if they were just products of the attempt his eyes were making to communicate with his brain.

Yoshi tried to move back through the doorway and away from where the house had fallen away, but he wasn't sure that he could, or if perhaps he already had.

"Alicia?" he whispered. "Franley?"

There was no answer. Timidly, he waved an arm out in front of him but found only emptiness and yet the emptiness responded. With no warning, no sensation, and no comprehension, the emptiness moved up over his arms and lay across his shoulders. It paused there for a moment, and Yoshi had a few seconds to contemplate the feeling. He thought it could have been a shawl, or an animal, but it had no weight and no warmth. Fleetingly, the thoughts subsided, as simultaneously, the emptiness grew towards his head and his chest. Then like a sleep that has been a long time coming, Yoshi ceased to be aware of anything at all.

He awoke on the carpet of the orchestra pit, the weave imprinting itself upon his face. The darkness had been replaced by what he perceived as an inferno. The stage floor was on fire. His body felt heavy, and all the emptiness had gone. He felt everything at an exacerbated intensity. Having awoken on his stomach it was with great difficulty that he managed to roll over onto his back. His face burning with the sting of the carpet's fibers, he looked up at the ceiling of the house awash in dancing ant-shaped shadows, their antennas swaying with the flickering of the fire. The rows of house lights were off. The stage lighting that hung out over the audience was also off. The only light came from the orange ferocity glaring in his periphery as he lay parallel to the stage. There was movement above what he perceived as flames. With a great deal of effort, he moved his head and caught sight of himself swaying on the catwalk.

It must be an illusion. That can't be me. Yoshi lay there feeling all his weight and all the weight of the moment, yearning to get up and to do something, to find the others, but unable to pull his eyes away from himself and what he might do, what he might see himself touch. *Don't do it. Don't touch the beams.* He willed his thoughts into what surely was not part of himself. There was nothing to feel from the Yoshi on the catwalk. There was no discerning connection, only abstract isolation.

"Franley? What happened? Where's Yoshi?"

He heard her calling out. *Alicia.*

He tried to lift himself from the floor, pulling his body to the right and wedging his elbow under his side. Leaning in with everything he could muster against the heaviness of it all, he pushed off the floor and almost fell over in the opposite direction with the ease and airiness of the reaction. As if gravity had reduced significantly, Yoshi nearly floated to his feet.

With his head swimming in the lightness, he cried out, glancing around and seeing only the piano that channeled something to Dugan. Flickering in shadow the tiger striped wood grain appeared to ripple and wave, the scrollwork of doves and ribbons mutating and shimmering into tusked creatures on parade. The quartz keys glinted in the firelight appearing hungry and eager to play. With a barely perceivable hush the orange glare from the stage began to shift and waver and now fade. He could perceive at last that it was not a fire at all.

There had been no answer to his cry. He tried again, shouting for Alicia with all the volume he could pull. The orange glare simmered to a dull visual hum against the floor. From the catwalk, movement caught his eye. Glancing up, he found his doppelganger was gone and instead two oddly long legs adorned with white sneakers swung playfully from below it, shoelaces flailing about. There followed a loud whoosh of air, shaking the whole of the house and the legs vanished as did the last of the orange light. Two faces peered down at him from the stage above.

Chapter 12

November 30, 2022

He had never been so happy to see her. With speed, Yoshi ran to the steps leading up from the orchestra pit, his half numb legs climbed without wavering. Alicia ran down from the stage to meet him at the top of the steps.

"Where did you go? I couldn't see you." He flung his arms around her.

"I didn't go anywhere," she whispered. "I was right there at the doorway the whole time, until you weren't. Then I heard Franley crying and saw that she must have gone around the other way instead. You—you were gone and so I didn't go through the door, but back up to her, to see what, why—whatever is going on? You were gone!"

"I don't know how I got in there. The emptiness took me." He pulled himself back and looked into her eyes. "I don't want to feel that again."

There was a mumbling, low rambling from the stage.

"They're trying to separate us. Don't you see? It's like what happened with you, Alicia. You and Mortimer got shut off from the rest of the group in his story, or your story. Whatever. The little imposter kid, or whatever he is, tried to put you in the orchestra pit. Didn't he? Now, you and Yoshi both disappeared as soon as the house door opened. I ended up on stage on a piece of masking tape. If I look closely, it probably has my name on it. And Maxwell? Well? What about him? He may well be dead for all we know or shoved in a closet.

Or maybe he's right here, but he can't see us. It's all contrived. All of it. I just want to go home."

Franley, pacing in the middle of the stage, fumbled with the flap of her purse and pulled out her list.

"I'm done with this nonsense." She began unfolding the paper and waving it in front of her, intending to drop it at her feet. There was a clatter from both wings. Every light went out.

"Nice. Very nice. It's oh so dark. Should I start crying again? Do you think you're going to make me angry?" she rallied out, the paper still clutched in her hand. She spun on her heels to check the space behind her.

"Don't let go," Yoshi whispered into Alicia's ear. "We will walk out of here together."

"What about Franley?" Alicia asked.

"We'll get her too, but don't let go of me," he answered.

"I didn't let go of you before, when you opened that door, but you were still—,"

"Hold on. Look."

Alicia could not see his face, but she saw the silhouette of his head turn toward the center aisle of the house. There was a faint familiar figure, striding in an easy-going trot. The tight white curls of his fur just barely visible in the washed motion of his gait. Beyond this spirit in the darkness, Alicia looked for the shadowed man in his proverbial row and found him seated there. His head shape and shoulder shapes rotated, leaning, looking to the back of the room from which a subtle blue light slipped across the seats and wafted toward Yoshi and Alicia. In her mind, Alicia heard a whisper saying, *Go. He's got this.*

The dog bounded onto the orchestra pit ledge and leapt to the stage, landing at stage left. As he did so, his ears perked and he turned his misty head to stage right. He gave a loud menacing bark that evolved into a growl. They watched a pronounced silver light flutter at the stage right curtain in response. Tendrils of softly blonde hair wisped outward with a wind that no one else could feel. The black velvet of the curtain vibrated a deep violet at the edges, flowing out and back, in sync with the hair.

With a small click, a beam of light shot out from the curtain, illuminating in magenta the space next to Franley, casting her image into shadow as she turned to face it.

With momentum that seemed unreal for any dog, he too shot across the stage, knocking himself into the back of Franley's knees, buckling her legs, and disappearing into the air as she went pummeling toward the floor. With the surprise of it all, her grip on the list in her hand loosened. As she fell forward, away from the beam, the purple ink on yellow paper fell upon it and was seen no more. Her knees thudded one after the other as she landed on her mark.

The overhead lights rippled, succinctly one by one, flashing back on and providing a steady brightness over the house. The stage was nothing more than empty, directly unlit space with a bewildered woman left to stare out at the vacant seats. The magenta light had gone, as had the silvery light and softly blonde hair, as had the dog, as had her list.

Franley remained on the floor. She rubbed her fingers over the strip of masking tape, the same one she had found a few moments before when she had screamed for Alicia, when she had smelled the cigars, and which she had just hit with her knees. It had all happened so fast, so much depth in the fragment of a minute hand's march. Time had passed as an incoherent accordion of inseparable events as stacked and fleeting as a heartbeat.

She had not really wanted to part with her list, and yet it was complexly a relief to feel that it had gone. This strange extension of herself—would it become like a phantom appendage? Would she still feel it and reach for it, though it were gone? She hoped there would be time for sorting that out later. For now, she must get up. Home was where she wanted to be, but every time she took a step in that direction something bad happened, or at minimum something she did not understand and did not want to experience again. Still, she knew she must get up.

They were calling for her as she moved her fingers away from the tape. Alicia and Yoshi were summoning her to go with them, to go now. She knew they were headed for the house doors that led into the lobby, and she knew she must follow. They were halfway up the stage left side aisle, in view, but she struggled to make sense of them and this vacant, normal, well-lit room. It was not that big, this place. It was not impressive by any historical standards. It just existed here in this tiny town and yet, it was filled to the brim with an electric charge that had no place in reality.

Franley looked at where the magenta light had come from and thought about the text Dugan had sent her only minutes ago. She thought about the single line in Mortimer's story where his professor friend says that Oren, or rather Dugan is, *a strange one, isn't' he? I caught him messing with the lights on the stage.* And hadn't it also been mentioned in that story that he was a professor of physics? She didn't know much about physics, and she didn't know much about theatrical lighting, but there seemed just one option left.

The floor stand she had maneuvered around when she was first brought on stage, held a single stage light, affixed. It sat in the place the magenta light had come from, and she could see no other lights around it. Pushing herself up from the floor, she hobbled over to it with a small, tired wince of pain in her knees. Careful not to be directly in front of the bulb, she positioned herself in the curtains behind it, grabbed onto the sides of the lamp head and swiveled it upward. Without allowing time to hesitate, she flipped it on.

"Look!" she cried out. "Look at where it can go."

The magenta beam shot directly up at the catwalk, flaying the handrails into tiger stripe shadows. There had been a misunderstanding. The catwalk beam did not make anyone disappear.

It was this beam of light that could transport whatever fell into its stream.

Franley turned to see if the others were paying attention. They had stopped at the door exiting into the house. Yoshi had one hand out, ready to push it open. They were looking up at her and she could see that they understood. Then without further ado, Franley switched off the light, grabbed hold of the neck of the floor stand, raised it into the air and smashed it down, bulb first. The smashing released a rounded gem, an amethyst, that rolled away and fell into the orchestra pit. The glass and metal of the bulb lay crumpled and flayed at her feet.

In the seconds immediately following the slaughtering, she waited for a slow clap, a dimming of the lights, a howling giggle, or the wafting of a cigar to play themselves three-dimensionally into her scene. There was only silence. Looking from the shattered bits on the stage floor, she stepped out from behind the curtain, turned back out to the audience, saw the shadowed man in his seat, and took a bow.

His phone lay on the pillow next to him, its last message to Franley still on the screen. In his bed across the sea, Dugan had fallen back asleep and dreamt for the last time of the room where he had first met her.

In the first dream, he had arrived in the room by a horse and carriage laden with bricks, the tiger striped wood grain legs of a piano, and matching wood grain doors. The carriage had faded into a violet, velvet curtain and she had met him in her strange, silver light, filling the space with cold brilliance. He thought she must be angelic. From this light she poured and soothed promises of what he could achieve. Such prominence and acclaim could and would accelerate his career on a grand and glorious scale. There would be witnesses and he would be admiral of his own reality. The ingredients for this success were easy and had already been mixed and poured in a town he could learn to call home. He just had to add a few final touches and she, his muse, would guide his hands victoriously. He had awoken from the dream with a rounded purple gem under his pillow.

This time the room was different. The silver light of her was jagged and thrust with anguish, causing the room itself to tilt at odd angles. There was no brilliance about her. She said nothing to him. There was no pouring out of sympathy, no promise of retribution. He pleaded with her to know what had become of their shared history. She would not even look at him. Simply she was there in all the horror of her truth and then she was gone.

He awoke, sobbing into his hands.

Chapter 13

November 30, 2022

She was almost to them. She was going home. Watching, as Yoshi made to push the door to the lobby open, hoping that it would not open into darkness and separation, Franley ran. She ran past the upholstered seats, vacant, with the exception of one. She ran past her fears, her curiosity, her anger, and she did not stop as the piano began to play. The notes rose from the silence in an immediate swell, a wave that lifted up from the deep without warning and pushed her onward as the lady sang.

They rang out as one voice, the piano and the lady in silver light and Franley realized they were one in the same. She did not see her, but she saw that Alicia saw. With one hand clutching Yoshi's shirt, tangling it in her fingers, Alicia was looking back, watching Franley bolting toward her, watching the lady in silver rise up from the orchestra pit from above the tiger-stripe wood grain piano that thundered and rolled and propelled the scene forward. It was not a familiar song, but something that felt as though it could only have been composed from this place itself, as if it could not have been heard anywhere else. They would all three discuss this one day and would only be able to describe it as outside of time but also restrained as if confined within a clap of thunder. If it were ever to be loosed of this restraint, it would deafen them all.

Yoshi took one glance back at the scene, grabbed Alicia's free hand with his, saw that Franley was within a stride of reaching them, and pushed the door open into the lobby. The room was as they left it, with one exception. The blue light buzzed from between the two swans on the fountain. Yoshi, keeping his tempo of step, made to keep going past, but Alicia yanked on his shirt still tangled between her fingers. She threw an arm out and caught Franley who had come up beside her.

A whisper lifted out of the buzz, out of the hum, and shaped itself within the spaces around them. It was soft and incomprehensible, yet it filled their ears with ease. It sing-songed its way around and around before fading out with a sigh. The blue light softened laterally and rippled out as if filling the basin with invisible water.

Franley opened her mouth to ask Alicia what that had been, to ask if it was the same as what had been in the office earlier, but before she could make a sound, one of the front doors slowly opened. A flashlight beam cast its way across their faces. Maxwell stood at the door.

"Maxwell?" Yoshi called out.

The officer lowered the flashlight and nodded.

"I went out the back, through the apartments. This place isn't right, but when I saw you weren't in the car, I figured you had come inside. I couldn't leave you here." He paused for a moment, glancing about. Then he added, "There's nothing else to see here tonight. Ms. Parker you can lock up." He tossed her the key, and with that he was back through the door, not staying a moment longer to see if they would follow.

Franley did as he suggested. She held the door open for the others and then quickly locked it behind them, dropping the key into her purse and smoothing the flap. Maxwell, already in his car and pulling away from the parking lot, waved as Franley hit the button on her fob to unlock hers. Alicia climbed into the back, but Yoshi stood by the passenger door for a moment, letting it hang open against his hip. His eyes trained on the theater. With her hand on the driver's side door handle, she turned to follow his gaze. He was focused on the oval window, with its stained lavender glass, and the iron frame with a single bar through the center.

"What is it?" she asked.

"Piezoelectric—," he said, "That stone that fell out when you smashed the bulb— I think, maybe? I don't know."

Franley pondered this for a moment, a little disturbed that Yoshi no longer seemed in a hurry to flee even though the theater was still right there before them. Then she asked, "Why do you think he wants to sell it? Dugan?"

"I don't think it's up to him," Yoshi replied, sliding into the passenger seat and slowly closing the door behind him.

There was silence for the first half of the drive back to Yoshi and Alicia's home. They drove out of the sleeping downtown, past porch lamps, dark side streets, and dimly lit yards scattered with children's toys. When Alicia broke the silence, she sounded calm and assured.

"They're just noise. I think. Just distractions," she said.

Franley glanced at her in the rearview mirror.

"They're real. I know. Distractions all the same, except the blue one," Alicia continued.

"Even the dog?" Franley asked with her eyes back on the road.

"Oh right, the dog. I do like that one." She leaned her head against the window and watched as the town turned into farmland mixed with small suburbs, drifting into thought about the barn Franley had said she used to see as a child, noting silently that a turn for their neighborhood would be about two fields up just past a barn with a dilapidated blue roof. A small buzz went off in her pocket. She was tired and didn't feel like taking it out, but she pulled out her phone anyway because she realized with a pang of guilt that it most likely was Louisa, whom they had all forgotten was waiting in the atrium of the Inventes.

A yellow paper? Appeared over the ledge and flew up at the window. Someone opened the window and retrieved it. This was about thirty minutes ago. Sorry. My cell service has been spotty tonight.

"Franley?" Alicia spoke up.

"Yes?" she replied.

"Franley, your list—someone has your list. Do you want it back?"

The Other Chapter 12

November 30, 2022

The night had been still. The sounds playing throughout it had not. The clamor of song orchestrated from beyond his comprehension had risen and fallen, faded, blurred, and burst forth again. Hamish held the sheets tangled between his fingers, refusing to let go of any minor tangible comfort. They did not hide, nor protect him, but they made him feel slightly less vulnerable.

The tiny digital clock on the top of the small television had kept the minutes faithfully, each one prolonged and dense. He had taken to staring at it, focusing on the passage of time, believing that it must not let him down. The minutes would turn into hours, and the hours would turn into daylight and the beams of morning would free him from this fear. He felt slightly embarrassed by it all, even in the midst of it. This was nonsensical to him, but it was real, as well. He wondered, as he had long ago, if something being real meant that it had to make sense? Did he really need to understand this to push past it? There was too much of the moment within him for any sort of decision. The uncertainty remained as did his grip on the sheets, until the rose lifted from the nightstand once again.

He caught sight of it in his periphery, then full on as it shot across the room and pelted the curtains and the window shade. Again and again it flung itself at the window. The song was rising in pitch to the point that Hamish wanted to cover his ears, but that meant he would have to let go of the sheets. Instead he ducked under them, pulling them tight around himself, over his head, and shuddering he lay there hoping to drown it all out without suffocating.

It was futile. The song made its way under the sheets with him. It billowed them without making them move. It caught him in his chest and pulled at his heart. The rose continued to pelt itself against the curtains. He could hear the softness of it, over the blaring, awful tune. The deep strangeness of it all was overwhelming. Driven by extinguishing resilience he flung the sheet from off himself and cried out, "WHAT! What do you want?"

He fumbled off the bed, half tangled in the sheets and stumbled across the quilt that had been knocked to the rug on the floor. Marching to the window with the quilt caught around his foot, he flung back the curtains, raised the shade, and the cream rose hovered for a moment before resting gently on his shoulder.

There, in strange suspension outside the window, was a partially folded yellow sheet of paper, the kind people used to keep on their office desks. No sooner had he calculated what it was when it hurled against the glass and two loud knocks, one following the other, pounded in the air around him.

He shook his head and took a step back. The rose nudged gently against his neck and motioned toward the window.

"Who are you?" he whispered. The rose rolled down his arm and into the palm of his wavering hand. It pushed against him until it unfurled his pointer finger outward toward the window.

Hamish shook his head again, but with a sudden burst and half a growl he lunged back at the window, the rose lifting itself away. He reached upward and outward and flipped the lock back. Then with the restless urgency of a man who is operating under compulsive duress, he raised the glass. As one pane slid against the other a voluminous shock of sound erupted around him, eviscerating the cacophonous song. It was the sound of shattering glass.

He jumped back and shielded his eyes, expecting there to be shards and debris, but when he pulled his arms away from his face, he found nothing in the silence but an open window with intact panes and the yellow paper lying on the floor with the cream rose on top.

Chapter 14

December 01, 2022

He had skipped the conference and gone instead to the location listed last on the yellow paper. Having spent the rest of the night pouring over its contents in the tranquil silence of the hotel room, Hamish knew he must meet the person behind the purple ink, if at all possible. They were like him. They had stories to tell.

When he opened his hotel room door and stepped out to find this location, he discovered the quartz room numbers from the door lying cracked and scattered in the middle of the space between his room and the opposite wall. He thought about picking them up, but instead, he simply double checked that the door had locked behind him.

He waited for the decent hour of 10 a.m. to arrive, before deciding at last to exit his car and approach the door of the brownstone. He felt a little awkward in his suit, but it was the only type of attire he had packed. The rose bushes with their golden, creamy petals rose up on each side of the porch bringing him a comfort and a welcome solace that he felt was not normal, but it did feel right, and he quickly forgot about his appearance.

He rang the bell and tried to guess the tune it played—familiar but not quite registering. The lyrics had almost come to him when the door opened and a brightly dressed, older gentleman with fluffy gray hair and matching eyebrows smiled out at him.

"She said you might be stopping by," he said, ushering Hamish inside upon seeing the yellow paper in his hands.

"She?" Hamish asked. "Is this hers?" He held out the list.

"Oh. Well, I guess they both said you might be stopping by."

The man smiled and extended his hand. "Mortimer Blackwood. Welcome to my home. Please excuse the absence of my friends, who undoubtedly are the actual reason you are here." He motioned to the list. "They've had a bit of a long night and Franley, whose list you are holding, has gone home, which is a little distance away. That's where she needs to be today."

"I'm not absent." Louisa entered from a doorway just off the side of the living room Mortimer had ushered Hamish into. "And I saw you receive that. Mortimer here would have too, but he slept through the whole thing and didn't get his messages until it was all over."

Before Hamish could say anything, she added, "I'm Lousia, by the way, and I was in the atrium, keeping an eye on your window ledge. I tried to call, but no one would ever pick up at the front desk and I wasn't about to go up there not knowing who was in that room, though I could tell someone was there because there was the blue light from your television. Also, I don't know if it works backwards, as in, I don't know if you can go from the ledge to the theater, or how that would even happen, but I would have called out to you and tried to stop you, had you tried—to go there that is."

Louisa and Mortimer were both talking rapidly and eagerly. Even though Hamish wasn't sure what they meant by going backwards to a theater, he felt as if he had stepped into the home of relatives he had not seen for a very long time. He had never met these two, of course, but here they were, welcoming him and speaking so freely as if they had known him since the day he was born. The man's last name was Blackwood, just like his, but surely there were a lot of Blackwoods in the world. It may just be a coincidence; except he wasn't sure he could believe in coincidences anymore.

He started to say that his television hadn't been on, but he was too slow to get a word in as they bustled around him mentioning names and events he had never heard of.

"She said you can keep the list. She doesn't want it back," Mortimer told him after they had settled into the living room chairs and graciously given him a cup of Earl Grey.

"Oh." Hamish frowned into the steam rising from his cup. "Do you think she would be willing to talk to me though? I've never had anyone, well until this moment, that I could talk to about things like this."

"Yes, I think she would be good with that. You should probably give her a day or so though. I will give her your contact information, if that works for you? That way she can call when she's ready," Mortimer replied.

Hamish nodded and asked for a pen. Louisa passed him one and a patch of sticky notes. He set down his tea on a side table and took them from her.

"I still don't understand, how I got this though." He motioned to the list he had placed next to him in the chair. "I don't understand any of what happened last night. There was this very strange song that kept playing and it was so swelteringly loud, but I felt like I was the only one who could hear it. Do you know if anyone from the Inventes has ever mentioned it?"

Mortimer shook his head. "No, but maybe it wasn't meant for anyone other than yourself."

"It just seemed like so much noise. It was hard to decipher anything from it," Hamish replied.

"Truth can prevail through the noise," Louisa said.

Mortimer smiled. "Yes, that is exactly the kind of thing you have to consider."

Hamish passed the sticky note with his contact information, and the pen back to Louisa and picked up the yellow paper from beside him. The purple ink was pressed into the page with a half neat, half scrawling penmanship. The loops and curls and dots and slashes, all bent and smiling up at him.

"Your name is Blackwood, too?" Louisa asked when she looked at the note Hamish had passed back to her, but her voice was so low when she said it that neither of the men heard her.

"She wrote that she saw something around your rose bushes. That's how I found you," Hamish said to Mortimer.

Mortimer sighed and looked suddenly weary and older than he had when he answered the door. "Yes, I think I knew Franley had, but for the life of me I can't tell you who she is. Not Franley, of course, but you know, the one who likes the roses. Dunwich roses, that's what they are. I do get the feeling she watches out for us though. Sometimes she comes around anyway, sometimes with the softest blue light. It's almost imperceptible. Maybe she's just saying hi, or maybe she's bored. Who can say?" He laughed suddenly, a small partly stifled one that he tried to cover by pulling his hand to his mouth.

"I think she's the one who tried to stop me from writing my Imagine Shadows story. Sometimes the backspace key would press down on my keyboard as I was typing it out. I could see it happening. I could watch the words disappear. Oh, it wasn't funny at the time, but now, now it is rather amusing."

"What is that? Imagine Shadows?" asked Hamish.

A smile spread across Mortimer's face. "Of course," he said. "Of course! Get ready, Hamish. You're about to find there are a lot of people out there just like you."

Louisa eyed Hamish, watching his features flex in anticipation as Mortimer headed off for the bookshelf at the far end of the kitchen. She noted the structure of his face and his slightly bushy, dark eyebrows. She smiled to herself as he raised them when taking a stack of magazines from Mortimer's hands, Mortimer having returned from the quest to retrieve them. Maybe there was something to it and maybe there wasn't, but names were important and that at least was something they had in common beyond the stack of stories before them.

"Hamish," she asked, "where did you say you were from?"

Epilogue

December 08, 2022

After putting away cereal bowls, kissing Liza and Billy on the top of their heads, and casting Bill a snarl face as she placed last night's empty wine bottle into the sink, Franley left with the promise of being back by two. The oven was off, but it beeped at her on the way out. She didn't even look back. She was on her way to meet Hamish and Lousia at the diner. Alicia had reserved them a table. Eager to meet these new friends, she had rushed out without her purse but at least had her car keys in hand. She ducked quickly back into the house to retrieve it and found it waiting in Bill's outstretched arms.

Arriving within sight of the town she had so recently fled yet was destined to return to—the selling of the theater must still be done—she noted a small sign off the side of the road, along a fence bordering a cow pasture. It was half covered in ivy, a plaque cast in iron, unkempt, and oxidized by time. Glancing at the clock on the dash and seeing that she had time to spare, she pulled off onto the shoulder of the road, crunching gravel and brambles of weeds.

Despite everything she had experienced she was still hungry for history and figured a quick look at the sign would not be a harm to anyone. Carefully, watching for other cars that may be coming down the road behind her, she got out and walked over to the post. The ivy had to be cleared away and the words were discolored, but still the script was clear enough.

1792

In honor of Della Rosetta Blackwood

Founder and Matron of Haydnston

Artist, Mother, Missionary,

Protector

Franley looked around at the faded pastures in the dawn of the December morning. Beyond their rough and parched horizon the town rose up, small, but still standing. She ran her fingers over the letters, jutting out from the plaque and then stepped back and looked down at the base of the post. Just in view behind the brambles was a small, cream rose, blooming against the cold.

About the Author

Stephanie Layton is fond of old places, gingerbread lattes, and stories that get a little weird. She has spent most of her life in Virginia, which features all of the above.

Read more at hauntedmauve.com.

.